letters

from a little little *texas*

COWDOG

letters
from a little little *Texas*
COWDOG

PHYLLIS CLEM

To order additional copies of this book, contact:
Xlibris
1-888-795-4274
www.Xlibris.com
Orders@Xlibris.com
798304

CONTENTS

Texas Bound

Hi Y'all,

My name's Kodi, and I'm the new head of security at the Clem Ranch in East Texas. *Y'all* is correct down here in Texas, isn't it? I'm not too sure since I was born in Missouri but got here as fast as I could. I'm joining two cats, two horses, and lots of black cows. I understand I'll get to help with those cows when I'm older, but right now I'm way too little to get around 'em. Mama says I need to stay away from the horses too cause they could step on me and not even know it. I guess I'll be bigger one day.

I mentioned there were two cats. One is a very big fellow named Mr. P. He's three times my size but seems friendly enough. He whispered to me that he wasn't really fat, just very fluffy. I don't know about that cause he seemed kind of fat to me. But I didn't say anything cause I didn't want to hurt his feelings and get off on the wrong paw so to speak. The other cat is named Little Bit and she is definitely smaller than the big guy. I don't think she and I will ever be friends though since she took one look at me, swatted me with her claws and ran up a tree. She hissed some things at me that I best not put in this letter either.

All in all things are going well in my new home. My folks give me lots of hugs and I have plenty of things to play with. They call me a little princess since they say I'm a privileged pup, whatever that means. They keep me busy with all sorts of activities too, and I sure sleep good at night. Something about a tired puppy being a good one.

One thing they like to do when they have some free time is chase a little white ball around a place called a golf course. I get to go along and ride in the cart. I've noticed that they sometimes like where that ball goes and sometimes not so much. It seems like a funny game to me, but if they like it then I like it.

We go for long walks everyday too and when we go check cows we ride in a machine called a mule. Those are fun times. When walking, I get to run and play and get in the ponds and creeks and get all wet and dirty. But that comes with a price cause then I have to get a bath before I get to come back in the house. Something about a wet, smelly puppy. I don't understand since I smell okay to myself. When we ride in the mule, I hang out the side and let the wind blow my ears and hair and think, "Man life is good."

I mentioned that I was supposed to stay away from those cows for now, but of course I didn't listen and got a swift kick in the side. I cried and cried and ran to Mama. She hugged me till I felt better, but then a few minutes later I was nosing around a culvert and disturbed a nest of red wasps and got stung all over my little belly. I cried again and made a beeline for Mama cause those things pack a wallop. She put something on the stings that helped, and I decided I'd had enough for one day and stayed on the deck for the rest of the afternoon. I guess I'm one of those pups who will have to learn things the hard way.

I've already been on my first trip if you don't count coming from Missouri to Texas. My folks like to watch professional bull riding so we went to an event right after I came here to live. We stayed in a hotel, and I met lots of people when we were out and about. Now I had to stay in the room by myself when they went to the event, but that was okay cause I had some of my favorite toys to keep me company as well as the TV to watch. I heard them say that our next trip will be to Branson and then to a cattle sale up in Arkansas. Sounds like my name should have been Gypsy.

Well, so long for now.

Your friend,

Kodi

Travel Adventures

Hi Y'all,

As I said 'life is good'. I just returned from that trip to Branson, Missouri and what fun I had. We stayed in a cabin that had a creek out back and I loved playing in that chilly water. I ran and ran and ran and put my head under the water and blew bubbles and had the best time. You know that'll tire you out pretty quickly though. My folks enjoyed all my antics and they laughed and laughed. It doesn't take much for them to get the giggles.

Of course they got in some golf while there with me riding shotgun in the cart keeping an eye out for pesky squirrels. For some reason golf courses seem to have lots of those fluffy-tailed critters; wonder why. I feel it's my duty to keep them in line since I am head of security at home. Why, one of them could run off with a golf ball and that would be a serious offense. So I stay on guard during the entire game. Maybe that why I'm tired afterwards—hmmmmm.

In the evenings my folks went to some of the shows Branson is famous for, but I stayed back at the cabin. That was okay though cause after a day being on guard duty and playing in that creek, I was pooped. A bed and some TV watching seemed like a good way for this little pup to spend the evening.

When we left there we went to Chimney Rock Cattle Company in Arkansas for a cattle sale. I met soooooo many folks and they all thought I was the cutest little thing. You know it's kind of hard to stay humble with all that attention and praise, but I'm trying to stay just plain ole Kodi and not expect to be called the Little Princess.

The ranch owners had two very big dogs called briards. Their names were Vegas and Edward and from my viewpoint they were huge. Try to imagine a pony with long hair. I wanted to make friends and play, but they decided to gang up on me and give chase. I ran under our truck and stayed there till Mama came to my rescue. Now don't get the idea I was afraid being that I do security work at our ranch, but two against one isn't fair when the one weighed in at fifteen pounds and they weighed in about ninety pounds each. Next time I see them I'll have grown some, so maybe things will be different.

All in all I had a great time. Since I'm getting close to the age of six months, I hear talk that I'll be visiting my doctor soon for a surgical procedure. Mr. P said he had his surgery at about that age and doesn't remember a thing. We'll see how it goes.

Later,

Kodi

Mr. P's Ears

Hi Y'all,

Looks like some holiday called Thanksgiving is just around the corner. Since this is my first one, I really don't know what it's all about, but I hear that it's a time for friends and family to get together for food and fellowship and to be thankful for their blessings. Mama said I might get some leftover turkey for a treat that day if I'm good. You know anything that involves the word *treat* sounds okie dokie with me.

Mr. P whispered something the other day about another big holiday coming up real soon and that I would probably get some new toys to play with. Now I really don't need anything since I'm a privileged pup, but I sure won't object to some new ones to scatter around the house. I love to drag all my stuff out, but I haven't learned to put my things away when I'm through playing. Guess I'll have to work on that.

He also said there'll be some different stuff in the house for a while that I'll have to leave alone or risk getting sprayed with the water bottle. He seems to speak from experience and he is older and wiser than me, or so he says. He said there'll be a tree with shiny things hanging from the branches and under that tree will be boxes and sacks filled with stuff called gifts. Since I'm just a pup, I'll probably get to find out about the water bottle, but I'm going to try to be on my best behavior during this time.

I mentioned earlier about having to have a little surgical procedure when I turned six months old and I got that done this past week. Like Mr. P said, I don't remember much since I was so groggy most of the time. I had to stay in the doggie hospital overnight, and I'll admit I didn't sleep very well even though I had one of my favorite toys and blankie to keep me company. I sure was glad to see my folks the next morning! And when we got in the truck to come home and the engine roared to life, I went out like a light. I'm not sore, but my stitches kind of itch. They're supposed to dissolve soon though.

I think Mr. P missed me even though it was only for one night. When I jumped out of the truck, he came over and rubbed and rubbed on me and swished his tail under my face. I think that's how cats show that they like you. That evening when we were on the couch, I made sure I gave his ears a good cleaning. He loves it, and since I have trouble holding my licker, that works out just fine. I clean his ears, he purrs loudly, closes his eyes, and all is right with the world. I just love that big ol' furry cat.

I sure had lots of energy the next day and was feeling good, so we went for a long walk. I got to get all wet and dirty and ran and chased everything that moved. Man, it felt good to be back to normal. Course that meant a bath too, but that was okay.

Well, so long for now,

Kodi

Christmas Spirit

Hi Y'all,

What a great time of the year this is with all the lights and decorations and presents under the tree. Did I mention presents? Well, I know one is for me even though I don't need anything, but I sure won't turn down something to add to my toy box.

Actually I got an early present last week. It's a round thing that flies through the air when my folks throw it and sure is fun to chase and try to catch before it hits the ground. It only takes a few runs after that thing to poop a pup out. I wonder if that's what my folks had in mind when they got it? Hmmmmmm.

By the way, I haven't bothered anything on or under that tree since it's been in the house. I believed what Mr. P said about being sprayed in the face with water. And I've noticed he doesn't go near it either when he's on his way to his favorite chair. I just suspect he's been on the receiving end of the water treatment but won't admit it.

I have learned the real reason we celebrate Christmas and that is it's Jesus's birthday. I'm not too sure who he is, but he must be very important to have a special day to honor his birth. I mean people from all over the world take time to honor him. I've also noticed that humans seem to have more of a giving spirit this time of the year and everyone seems happy. Too bad it can't be like that all year long.

Even Little Bit must have the Christmas spirit cause she's been somewhat nicer to me lately. Even though I still chase her up the tree out back when I get the chance, she hasn't hissed as many unkind things at me. Mama says we've got to learn to get along, but I don't think that'll ever happen. She was never destined to be my good buddy like Mr. P.

Well, enjoy the holidays and we'll see what the new year brings.

Merry Christmas,

Kodi

Happy New Year

Happy New Year Y'all,

You know I'm kind of glad this holiday stuff only comes around once a year 'cause I'm pooped from all the activities. Now don't get me wrong, I had lots of fun and who can complain about presents. I even got to visit and play with my doggie cousin Kate. She's a real pretty bird dog and is lots of fun to be with. She chased me and I chased her till our tongues were hanging out. The weather was kind of drippy that day, but we still had a good time. That was our first playdate, but we liked each other from the get-go. Now she didn't know anything about being a cowdog since her thing is bird hunting, but we still had things in common. She gets to ride in the mule out in the pasture, has a nice bed in the house to sleep on and has a cat for a best friend. You know, things like that.

Later on a friend of Mama's brought her pal named Lola out for a visit. We had a grand time too. Now she's a city girl and sure didn't know what to think of the cows and horses, nor did they know what to think of her. She's a goldendoodle with lots of curly blonde hair and those cows sure gave her some strange looks. They're more used to seeing a little cowdog with a wiggly butt, namely me.

I understand that since it's a new year, you're supposed to make resolutions. I guess mine will be to not bark at everything unless it's really necessary and to learn the language of *mooooo*. That's going to be necessary in my future line of work. Mr. P said his was to keep on the same schedule of sleeping and eating as much as possible. I think he has that down pat already. He's kind of like a comfy overstuffed chair—ya just gotta love him.

All in all life is good!

So long. Try and stay warm in the cold days to come.

Kodi

I'm Famous

Hi Y'all,

Can you believe it? A picture of me and my favorite stuffed toy—the famous bucking bull Little Yellow Jacket—was published in the *PBR Magazine* this month! I was just a little tyke when Mama got this toy for me when we were at a PBR event down in San Antonio. From day 1, he was my favorite thing to drag around the house and sleep with. When LYJ was on the bull riding circuit he was ridden very few times, but when I got a hold of him, he met his match so to speak. He's been retired from my toy box for a while now since all his stuffin' came out and I'll admit that I may have had something to do with that, but I sure remember all the good times we had together.

Mama said I couldn't get the big head now just cause I was being seen by folks all around the country. But it sure is fun to look in that magazine and see my cute self staring back. Don't worry—I'll remain just plain ole Kodi to all of you guys even though I'm now kind of famous.

So long for now. Don't be surprised if you see me in some other magazine cause you know how it is when you're a celebrity. Someone is always taking a picture of you.

Kodi

Snow in Texas

Hi Y'all,

Man, oh, man, have I been having fun! It snowed about eight inches last night while I was sleeping. When I woke up and went outside, my whole world was white. I didn't know what to think since I'd never seen any of that cold stuff. I'm only eight months old, and snow in this part of Texas, well, let's just say that it doesn't happen very often.

After all the critters got fed, we headed out for our morning walk. Since I'm still kind of little, I wore out pretty quickly just trying to run in that stuff. When we got back to the house, Mama put me in some warm water to thaw out, and then I got a good towel drying. I sure was ready for my breakfast and a nap by the fire. I played in the snow for several days, but then it started to melt, and everything was brown and muddy. That meant I got my feet washed several times a day since Mama has a thing about clean floors.

My horse friends, Sug and Misty, seemed to like the white stuff as well. I noticed them running through the pasture they stay in with their tails up high and snorting and blowing through their noses. I could tell they were having a grand ol' time.

Now Mr. P and Little Bit didn't seem to care for the cold stuff much. I've learned in my short lifetime that cats generally don't like the cold, and they sure don't like getting their feet wet. Don't know why. That's just the way it is. And I've noticed something else. They seem to use their tails kind of like a warm scarf. Now I don't have one and that's why my kind are called wiggle butts, but Mr. P and LB have real fluffy ones. When Mr. P curls up for one of his long naps, he kind of wraps it around his face and ears to, I guess, help keep him warm. Seems like a pretty useful thing to have on a cold day.

I sure hope it'll snow again, but I guess we'll just have to wait and see what Mother Nature has in store for us the rest of this winter.

Stay warm,

Kodi

Numero Uno

Hi Y'all,

If you say, "Happy birthday," real loud, I bet I will hear you since I can hear the treat jar open even if I'm at the other end of the house.

I can hardly believe that I'm one year old. Mama still calls me a little princess even though I don't really know what that means, but I kind of get the idea that the world revolves around me in the Clem household. I got some new chewy toys and a red rubber thing called a Kong that I just love. When my folks go out for the evening and I stay at home, they'll put some peanut butter inside that thing and I have to use my licker to get that wonderful stuff out. It takes a while, but I manage to get every little bit. Whoever invented that thing sure gets my paw of approval.

You know from day one here on the ranch, I've been best buds with Mr. P, but not so much with Little Bit. You might say I'm not very high on her list of favorite things. I know I chase her up trees and to the barn all the time, but I think she really enjoys the chase. I mean, isn't that a pretty normal thing for me to do? I bet that dogs chased cats on Noah's ark. Anyway, I'd chase Mr. P now and then, but he's not really into the running thing, so I just give his ears a good cleaning and look for something that actually moves faster than a snail to chase.

Now there are other furry critters that I love to chase, and that's squirrels. And there are hundreds of those furry-tailed things on our golf course, but I don't get to go after them very often. Something about bad manners and all, but the other day, one was right in front of our cart and Daddy said, "Oh, what the heck, go for it, Kodi!" So off I went. I put that thing up the nearest tree in 1.2 seconds, but then it started saying unkind things to me and even threw down some pine cone shavings. I thought how rude, but maybe I deserved it since I did make him run up that tree. Knowing me though, I'll do it again every chance I get.

I've been on the road some lately to cattle sales and the like. A few weekends ago we went out to Abilene to an event called the Western Heritage Days. Boy, that was a fun outing. I met lots of people and dogs too. I actually got tired of being hugged and having my wiggly butt sniffed, but that's life when you're as cute as I am. One lady remarked that my hair was black and shiny just like Elvis's was. Never heard of that dude, but I guess he must have been famous maybe like me since I was in a magazine.

I heard we're going to Branson again and then to the cool mountains of Colorado pretty soon. I'm looking forward to that trip since it's already gotten too warm for my taste here at home. Thank goodness for air conditioning. Since I am a cowdog, I have to work out in the heat some, but on those hot days, it sure feels good to come inside and stretch my little belly out on the cool tile floor. On those days, you can almost hear my belly saying, "Ahhhhh."

So long for now. I'll let you know about those trips that I mentioned the next time I write.

Kodi

Vacation Time

Hi Y'all,

In my last letter, I mentioned we were going to the mountains when it got real hot here in Texas. Well, we just got back from that trip and may I say WOW. It was so nice and cool that we didn't even have to use the AC. Most of our time was spent in Telluride, Colorado and I sure met lots of nice folks and dogs too. Most of those I came across were either Labs or golden retrievers, which made me feel kind of small. I even met two Bernese mountain dogs, and were they ever big, kind of like my friends from Arkansas, Vegas and Edward. When I saw them coming down the street with their person, I thought they resembled me—you know, same markings and hair color—but then I noticed they had tails and heard Mama say what breed of dog they actually were. They were so big I could have easily walked under them.

We stayed at a condo up in the mountain village above the town itself, and it was a great place to hang out. There were plenty of places to get out and run and play and then a nice patio where I could have some nap time. Boy, that mountain air will take the zippidy out of your doodah after some playtime too. Mama said it was because we live at 200-foot elevation back in Texas and where we were staying was about 9,500-foot elevation. Didn't understand what she was talking about, but I sure could feel the difference. There was one downside to all this and that was a monstrous thing called a gondola. To get to town the easy way, you had to ride that thing, and the idea of getting on that moving monster scared me barkless. From day one when we got there and were unloading luggage and that thing passed over us, I thought it might just scoop me up and carry me off. Imagine how I felt when I found out we would be riding it from time to time. Daddy actually had to carry me on it the first time. My heart was racing so fast, I thought it might jump out of my chest. As it started moving, I decided all was okay and relaxed a bit and tried to enjoy the beautiful scenery. I heard someone say their dogs loved to ride it but not me. Now I don't want you to think I'm a scaredy cat since I am head of security at home, but I think there are some things that you need to be a little wary of and a gondola is on that list.

While there, we did some hiking and relaxing, and of course, my folks got in a few rounds of golf. I rode along and kept a watchful eye out for squirrels. I saw a few but didn't get to chase any. I did discover a new critter we don't have here in Texas, and that's a marmot. There was a family of them living in the rocks about the seventeenth tee box, and they sure fussed at me when I walked up. They dove back into their rocky home when I gave them my cowdog stare. I also met up with some little fast furry creatures called chipmunks. We were out hiking, so I did get to give chase, but they retreated to their underground home. I dug around where I smelled them go under, but all I got was a muddy face and paws. Course you know what that meant—yes, a good washing when we got back to the condo.

I had a great time and am ready for our next adventure. Who knows what critter I might meet up with?

Kodi

On the Road Again

Hi Y'all,

Maybe my name should be Gypsy since I just got home from another road trip. This time, we went to Memphis, Tennessee, to attend another PBR event. I heard that that's the home of Elvis and the blues, but I really don't know who he is or what's meant by the blues. Everyone says I have Elvis hair, so I guess it's only right I should go there.

It sure was hot unlike Colorado where it was so nice and cool. In the evenings, I stayed in the hotel room while my folks attended the event, but after a hot day on the golf course and a long walk, I was very content to stay where the AC could be turned down to low freeze.

You know it's kind of funny how my folks search for just the right TV program for me to watch while they're out 'cause as soon as the door closes and I get the bedcovers and pillows just to my liking, the only thing I watch is the inside of my eyes. The bad thing about snoozing while they're out is I'm ready to play when they get back, but then they're ready for some sleep. I usually go back to sleep pretty quickly though when the lights go out. Although sometimes I sneak up and give them a good face licking then make a hasty retreat and konk out.

I got to meet one of my folks' favorite bull riders when we were coming back from a walk. He and his family were staying at the same hotel as us. He sure was nice and thought I was the cutest little thing; course I'm getting used to that. He bent down and gave me a pat on the head and a hug, and I got the wiggles and just couldn't stop my backside; I guess I'm no different than any female when a cute guy pays attention to us. We wished him good luck that evening and headed back into the hotel. I was ready to get out of the heat and into the AC. I sure hope our next trip will be back to somewhere cool!

Later,

Kodi

Armadillos

Hi, y'all,

I got to thinking that in my recent letters, it sounds like all I do is ride around in a golf cart, chase squirrels and Little Bit, or go on trips, but that's not really true. I keep a close watch on what goes on here at the ranch. If anything seems out of order, then I have a bark that signals my folks to come running. I mean a stray cat could have wandered into the yard, you know, things like that. When we're out checking cows or taking a walk, I make sure to keep an eye out for invaders like armadillos. Have you ever seen one of those things? They're strange looking with little heads and beady eyes, and what about that thing on their backs? It's hard as a rock. But if you chase one of them, then you'll discover those short legs of theirs can really move, and they don't run up trees but dive into holes in the ground. And you can stay there as long as you want, and they're not going to come back out either. I'm not too sure what their purpose is here on earth, but I guess God has something in mind when he created them. He sure seems to have a sense of humor regarding some of the critters I come across. I mean I'm as cute as can be but armadillos, not so much.

There's not much that needs my attention regarding cows this time of the year. They spend most of their time grazing grass and raising their young'uns. I go help check on them daily, but I think that'll change in the coming months when I learn to work with them. That's why I need to learn to speak *mooooo* so I can communicate with them better. That'll definitely help me with my work. Since I am a cowdog, I sure don't want you to think I'm not doing my job as head of security around here.

So long,

Kodi

Swollen Head

HI Y'all,

Yep, I finally did it. Stuck my nosey snout where I shouldn't have and got it stung by something. We were out doing yard work—well, my folks were working, and I was supervising from the shade tree when Mama noticed me running around like crazy, trying to rub something off my nose. I wasn't having any luck either. When she got me to stop, my head was already starting to swell up. She ran inside and called my doctor and was told to look for blood—none visible—and then to give me a little pink pill called Benadryl every eight hours till the swelling started to go away.

Man, I looked terrible for the next couple of days and felt just as bad. I mean my head was twice its normal size, and I couldn't stop drooling. Those little pills made me sleepy too, so I spent most of my time under Daddy's desk where it was dark and cool and no one could see me. Eventually I started to look like my cute self again.

Mama had just said that if I got through the summer without getting stung or snake-bit, it would be a miracle cause I'm always poking my head into places I shouldn't. I guess you could say I never met a hole or culvert I didn't like.

I'm going to try to be good and stay out of harm's way, but knowing me, I'll probably do something like that again.

Later,

Kodi

Rocky Mountain High

Hi Y'all,

Guess what? Since my last letter, I haven't been in any trouble, nor have I stuck my nose where it doesn't belong. I know that's surprising, but it's true.

And we just got back from a trip to Ruidoso, New Mexico. Mama's birthday is in September, so that gave us a good reason to go somewhere, not that my folks need one. As I said, my name should have been Gypsy.

The weather was nice and cool, and everything was green unlike here at home since we've kind of been lacking in the rain category lately.

Course you know my folks got in some golf with me riding shotgun. When we play at courses other than the one we play at regularly, I don't get to get out and run, but at one point, Mama said to go ahead and have some fun. There were four guys in front of us who seemed to be having some trouble keeping their balls in the fairway as the game is supposed to be played, so that made us do a lot of waiting. We were on the seventeenth tee box, and no one was around, so I jumped out of the cart and put the *run* in *running*. I ran and ran and rolled in the cool green grass till my tongue was hangin' out and my wiggly butt was draggin'. Man, was that ever fun!

We also did some hiking up at the ski area. I got to be off leash and explore to my heart's content. I sniffed every bush I came to and waded in the cold mountain streams. *Brrrr*, that's some chilly water. There were other folks out hiking too, and I made sure they got a big Texas howdy cause I'm the friendly sort, you know. That always means a good hand or face washing since I can't hold my licker very well.

Love these fun trips and who knows where we'll head next.

Kodi

The Helicopter Incident

Hi Y'all,

Hurray, summer is finally over, and fall has arrived! I really don't like hot weather, so these cooler days and nights suit me just fine. I get kind of frisky when the temps drop some and have lots more energy, not that I don't have quite a bit anyway. Even Mr. P moves around a little more when it gets cooler. Now don't go getting excited cause I said "a little." He's not going to exert himself too much no matter the temperature.

I know you'll be surprised by this, but we just got back from a trip to my home state of Missouri. I'm all Texan now, but it was fun to visit the area where I was born and spent the first six weeks of my life, not that I really remember much about it. I do remember I had lots of brothers and sisters, and I hope they hit the jackpot when it comes to their forever families like I did.

We stayed in the same cabin as the last time, but the creek I played in was dry, so no fun to be had there. The stairs made up for no water to splash in though. I ran up and down over and over, and Mama said I sounded like a herd of horses at full gallop. I would run up to the top of those stairs then race back down till my tongue was hanging out and my little butt was draggin'. Then I'd plop down on the cool floor, rest up, and do it all over again. Needless to say, sleeping at night was not a problem.

I did have a bad experience, and I don't mind admitting that I was pretty scared. You may remember the evil gondola I disliked while in Telluride this past summer. Well, that thing met its match in a scary machine called a helicopter. One day, I was out with my folks, and one of those whirring things landed in a field right next to where we were walking. It scared the bejesus out of me! My folks tried to assure me that all was okay, but all I wanted to do was let my little legs see how fast and far they could run. Course I was on a leash, so I wasn't going anywhere fast. There's something about things over my head that I just don't like. I guess my mind thinks they'll swoop down and carry me away. Mama said that lots of people ride around in those weird-looking airships. I thought well not me, no way, nada. I'll just stay here on solid ground.

Anyway we had a good trip, but I'm staying away from gondolas and helicopters if I can.

See you down the road,

Kodi

A New Friend

Hi Y'all,

Do you remember the trip we took last year to Chimney Rock Cattle Company up in Arkansas? That's where I met Vegas and Edward for the first time. If you recall, I was kind of scared of them since they're such big dogs, and I'm kind of on the little side. Well, they still live there, but this time, Edward actually wanted to play some rather than chase me under the truck. We ran and ran, but I was too fast for him, and he tired of our game pretty quickly and went to find his mom. I did make a new friend though, and her name was Zena. She's a German shepherd who lives in Little Rock, and her folks are good friends with the owners of this place. She's my age and had lots of energy like me, so we had a grand time running and playing. She has real long legs and could keep up with me when we were running straight away, but when it came to changing directions in a flash, I could turn on a dime and give her nine cents change. When you're a little cowdog, you've got to be quick so as not to get kicked.

I know you're not supposed to want something someone else has, but Zena had the prettiest pink collar with her name on it in shiny stones. I think I'm going to put that on my Christmas wish list in the *numero uno* spot. I think one in red would look real nice next to my shiny black hair, don't you?

There was another dog there from Dallas that I sort of got to know. She was a mini schnauzer named Samantha, and she had the prettiest silver hair. I asked if it was naturally that color, but she just winked and said only her hairdresser knew for sure. I didn't know what she meant by that cause I'm a country dog and Mama does my hair. She wasn't much interested in playing with me or Zena though; I guess we were a little rowdy for her city ways.

We were there for a cattle sale since that's the business my folks are in, and my Daddy bought one. Actually he only bought part of a cow— don't really understand how you can do that, but she must have been pretty special cause seemed like from the bidding that everyone else wanted that part. Our part didn't actually come home with us, and for that, I was grateful cause I was kind of worried about having to share the back seat of the truck with a cow for the long ride home.

Had another good trip and will look forward to seeing my friends the same time next year.

So long,

Kodi

Patience and Pecans

Hi Y'all,

Don't you just love how nice and cool the days have become? It won't be long till we'll have a fire burning in the evenings, and I do love that. Now when the weather is just cool, my folks have a fire in the outside pit, but when it gets cold, then they'll burn one in the den fireplace. After a busy day of cow work or just being an energetic pup, there's nothing better than a snooze by a warm fire.

And this cool weather has Mr. P acting a little friskier. Now Little Bit is always on the move even when I'm not chasing her but the big guy, not so much. The other day, I actually saw him out stalking a bird. When it flew away, he even chased after it a bit. But then he stopped as if to say, "What am I doing?" and headed off to his food bowl for a pick-me-up and then to a comfy spot for one of his long naps. You know, if he chased birds or anything a little more often, he might not be so fat, uh, fluffy. Just sayin'.

Now that the cool has come, it's the time of the year for the leaves to start falling. And they are for sure. It's fun to find a big pile and run through them scattering them in the wind. That is unless that's a pile Mama has just raked up, and then I get my name called rather loudly. Oh, and the pecans are falling too, and I have learned just how luscious those tasty nuts are. I mean that stuff is good! I can crack them open with my teeth, but when I don't feel like it, I take one over to Daddy and let him crack it for me. All in all, he's been pretty easy to train to give me what I want. Sometimes he even sneaks me treats from the table when Mama's not looking. I think that's a no-no, but if it makes him happy, then who am I to deny him that warm fuzzy feeling?

Lately I've come to the conclusion that patience is not one of my virtues. When I get my hair brushed, Mr. P always wants his done at the same time. He'll get up on the table and try to push me out of the way. Mama gets both of us done, but I like to be first and not have to wait my turn. When I push him out of the way, he always walks off and looks back at me as if to say, "Talk to the tail, wiggly butt." I guess since he sleeps twenty-three hours out of the day, waiting is no big deal to him.

And I've been tempting fate some lately, too. When I'm out running in the pastures, I like to run real close to the cows' back heels. I know I'll probably get a swift kick one day, but I kind of like living on the edge. Playing it safe all the time is no fun. Course I'll probably change my mind the day a hoof connects with my nose, but for the time being, just call me Kodi aka Danger Pup.

I hear that Thanksgiving is coming soon, so I'm hoping for some more of those turkey treats. I bet if I cock my head just right and bat my lashes, I'll get some. My folks fall for that routine every time.

Later,

Kodi

Trouble Squared

Hi Y'all,

Today seemed like my day for getting into trouble. My mischievous nature caused me all sorts of problems. One of which was getting my head stuck in the dishwasher rack. I've developed a bad habit of sticking my head in the dishwasher when the door is open to see if there's any food left on the plates that I can lick off. Well, this morning, I did just that, and my collar got hung on the lower rack. When Mama turned around to add dishes and said, "Kodi, NO!" I tried to back away as fast as I could, but that rack wouldn't drop off. I kept trying to get away from that thing, but it kept following me wherever I went. It was clanking, and I was yelping, and Mama was trying to catch up with me as I drug it, plates and all through the den. Finally it came loose, and I took off and hid under the bed. I just knew I was in for a scolding, but then I heard my folks laughing about the whole thing, and I knew I was forgiven. And believe it or not, no plates were harmed during this fiasco, just my dignity.

That wasn't the end of my exploits for that day though. As I said, I seemed bound and determined to push my luck in the trouble department. After the dishwasher rack was put back in place, we headed for the golf course. When we get to the ninth fairway, I usually get out of the cart and run and play a bit while my folks are putting out. Well, for some reason, I had a desire to run in sand, and close by were two sand traps. I just couldn't help myself and got in those traps and ran back and forth and back and forth, scattering sand everywhere. My folks were yelling "NOOOOOOO!" but I just couldn't stop since I was having so much fun. Now when you leave footprints in a golf sand trap, you're supposed to rake them out to leave it smooth for the next player. Well, I sort of left more than a few prints, and you know who had to rake them smooth and since I can't hold a rake in my paws, it fell to my folks to do the work. They weren't laughing this time either, and I was confined to the cart for the rest of the game.

I'm going to try to be on my best behavior till at least tomorrow. I'll let you know how long being good lasts.

Till then,

Kodi aka Trouble Squared

Moooooooo

Hi Y'all,

Guess what? Christmas is almost here again! Our tree is up and all decorated with petty shiny things. I learned from Mr. P last year that I should leave that tree and the stuff under it alone, and I did just that, which I know surprises you what with my mischievous nature and all. I know some of those presents are for me, but I'll have to wait till Christmas Day to see what they are. That's sure hard since patience is not one of my virtues as I've said before.

I finally found out what I was born to do. Now you know I love to travel, ride on the golf cart, chase squirrels and Little Bit, eat pecans, and clean Mr. P's ears, but my real talent is moving cows from one place to another. I knew from my first day here that eventually I would get to help work cattle, and that time has finally come.

Since it's winter, the cows pretty much have to eat hay since their grass is all brown, but Daddy planted some special grass that grows in cold weather. The cows get to graze on it for a few hours each day, and then they have to be moved back to the field where their hay is. That's where yours truly comes in. I bark and get behind them and tell them to get moving, or I'll nip their heels. Now I've had to learn their language, *mooooo*, so I can do my job well. If you don't speak *mooooo*, you may think all *mooo*s mean the same thing, but you're wrong. It all depends to whom the *mooooo* is directed. For instance, they could be saying things like "Nice day, isn't it?" or "This sure is some tasty grass we're grazing on" or "Did you get a look at the new bull cause he's a hottie?" When the *moooo* is directed at their calf, they might be saying, "Stay put, little one, and I'll check on you shortly." But in my case their *moooooo*s always mean the same thing: "If you get any closer to my back heels, little dog, I'm going to kick you into next week." They don't always want to leave that grass and get kind of irritated when I make them. Anyway I pay them no mind and keep on with my job, and I'm getting real good at it too. I may be little, but I'm a bona fide cowdog, and I take that title seriously.

Merry Christmas to one and all! Oh, I'll let you know about those presents.

Kodi aka the Little Cowdog with a Wiggly Butt

Sleepy Thoughts

Happy New Year Y'all,

Hope your holidays were all you wished for. I got a new chewy bone so big, it should keep me busy for a while, and I got a new stuffed bear that's super soft. Sure will make a good sleeping partner. I was wishing for a new collar with shiny stones that spelled out my name but didn't get it. Maybe that'll be my special birthday present in a few months.

I can't believe it but it has snowed again! It's only my second winter here in Texas, and we've had another big snowfall. I absolutely love playing in the white stuff. I run and try to catch it as it falls and put my nose in it and run and make tunnels. What fun! Mr. P doesn't seems to enjoy it like I do. He's sort of all grouchy about the whole thing.

The downside to all this is it's *cold*! I'm sure glad I get to come inside and get all warm and toasty by the fire. Even Mr. P and Little Bit stay in more when it's as cold as this spell has been. But my girls and the horses have to stay out in it so they get extra feed every day. Now Sug and her daughter Misty have barn stalls to go in, and I notice they do more often when the weather is this nasty. I said "my girls" when I referred to the cows cause that's what I call them now since we've developed a working relationship. I did take time to learn their language, and I think they respect me for doing so. Course one of these days, I may still be on the receiving end of a swift kick to the nose since I do get kind of close to their heels when moving them around. Mama says it's bound to happen, and I'll let you know if it does even though it will be embarrassing.

The other day, I came back from work and decided to have a little snooze before Mama cleaned me up to come inside. It was cold, but the sun was out, and it felt oh so good on my fur. As I lay there in the warm sunshine, I got to thinking that it's about time for Misty to get her education under saddle. She's about my age—two—and already knows how to stand to have her hooves trimmed and how to walk beside my folks when she's haltered, but now it's time for her to go away to kind of a horse boarding school for several months to learn some new things. I got to wondering if Sug will miss her. And then I got to thinking about my brothers and sisters whom I left behind when I was just six weeks old. Do they get to do the job they were bred for? Do they get to sleep in the house in a warm, comfy bed? Is a fat, uh, fluffy cat their best friend? Do they get to travel and meet new people and their dogs? Just wondering.

About then, the warm sun caused my brain to go numb, and I dozed off, so I guess I find out those answers later.

Stay warm during this cold spell,

Kodi

Brrrrrrrr

Hey Y'all,

How's it goin' in your neck of the woods? Man, oh, man, but it's been cold here. It hasn't gotten above freezing all week, and that's kind of unusual for this part of Texas. Now I like cold weather over hot any day, but this spell has been a little much even for my taste. Whoever mentioned this global warming thing hasn't been outside lately.

Mr. P and Little Bit have been staying in the house a lot, and that's right up fluffy boy's alley. He gets in his favorite chair and sleeps the day away. He can stay in the same position for hours. The other day, I went and checked on him just to see if he was still breathing, and he opened one eye and gave me that look that says, "Go away, dog. You're bothering me." I could never stay still for that long cause I have too much energy. LB has taken the whole staying-in-the-house thing in stride. She'd rather be outdoors where she can roam, but I think this cold snap has shown her that fireside napping isn't so bad.

She and I have been on pretty good terms lately. Truth be known, I decided I might best make peace with her when she's indoors at least cause she put the whup on me the other day. I startled her when she was coming around the corner, and she let me know it was in the best interest of my good health if I left her alone when inside. She said it with her claws extended too. Now outdoors all bets are off; if she runs,

I'm giving chase. Course I don't know what I'd actually do if I caught her. I kind of have the feeling I'd let go pretty quickly cause she has good control of those things at the end of her paws. I mean she might swat my pretty face, and I might have to have plastic surgery to repair the damage.

Well, so much for lying by the fire. The sun has come out, and the snow is melting some, so it's time to go check on my girls again, and maybe I'll get one of those cubes Daddy feeds them when it's extra cold.

You know I'm a lucky pup. I have a job I love, a warm house, folks who love me, friends, and plenty of treats. It just doesn't get better than this.

Stay warm, and Mr. P says, "Think spring."

Kodi

Yummy

Hi Y'all,

I've discovered something wonderful and wanted to share my findings with all of you. It's a tasty morsel that comes from the microwave and is called *popcorn*. I actually discovered it a while back but am afraid I'm getting addicted to it.

My folks like to have some to snack on when bull riding is on TV, and I make sure I get my fair share or more if I bat my lashes just so. When Mama goes to the cabinet and gets a bag out and puts it in the microwave and it starts going *pop- pop-pop*, I can't tear myself away. When she opens the bag, my mouth starts drooling till I get that first little bite. I think I would trade in all my toys for the white stuff. I might even trade in Mr. P, well, LB anyway, just to get some of those luscious white morsels.

I wonder what else is out there that I have yet to discover in the way of treats. Hmmmmmm.

So long, gotta run cause I just heard that wonderful sound. Give this stuff a try and see if you agree with me.

Kodi

Funky Smell

H I Y'all,

I've heard tell that if you don't like the weather here in Texas, then just wait a minute, and it'll change. Well, change it did; a short time ago, the temperature wasn't above freezing all week, and now it feels like springtime. You may remember that Mr. P said we should think spring, and now it seems to be here. The grass is greening up, which will make my girls happy, and some trees even have buds on them. After several months of brown grass and bare tees, the green sure is nice.

I've discovered a new smell called chicken litter. Now for those of you who don't know what that is, I'll explain. It comes from chicken droppings and helps grass to grow and get real green. But the downside to this kind of fertilizer is it's funky smell. The other day I was out walking in the pasture with my folks, and as I rounded a corner to get to another field, I spied some big brown mountains that weren't there the day before. My curiosity got the best of me, so I went and checked them out. When I got close, the smell just about knocked me over. Sitting on top of those smelly mountains were two buzzards I'd seen hanging around before. I think their names are Herkel and Jerkel, but I'm not real sure since Mama says I shouldn't get close to them as they have nasty habits. Anyway holding my breath, I got closer and asked how they could stand to sit on top of something that smelled so funky. They just laughed and said, "Silly little dog, this smells like a bed of roses to us." I kind of wondered if they had bad colds or something and their smellers weren't working just right. Now leftover steak or popcorn smells great to me, but this stuff, *no*. And I don't mean to be rude, but God must have had some spare parts lying around and put them together and came up with a buzzard. Like armadillos, they are not one of his prettiest creations.

About then, my folks got close and whistled for me to join them so I bade goodbye to the Texas turkeys as they're called. Mama said she would be glad when that stuff got spread out and rained on so the smell would go away. Amen to that!

Be doing a little traveling as of late to some cattle events. I sure enjoy these outings since I get so much attention. There were some little kids at one event who even liked sharing their food with me. Now if it makes a young'un happy to share their hotdog or candy bar with me, then who am I to deny them that pleasure? Course when Mama saw the sharing, I had to come join her. Something about me getting sick from chocolate. I didn't, and it sure was good.

So long for now. Hopefully rain will be on the horizon so that smell will go away.

Kodi

Mouse Ears

Hi Y'all,

Spring has sprung, flowers are in bloom, March is here, and April will be soon.

Hey, I'm a poet and didn't know it. Ha ha!

When we were out checking cows the other afternoon, I heard Daddy say that this nice weather made him want to wet a hook. Now I've been head of security and all-around best bud for almost two years now and have never seen him go fishin' even though we have lots of ponds. I think his favorite way to fish is at a restaurant where it's cooked and brought to the table, just saying.

Mama said when she was a little girl, a neighbor of theirs loved to fish and hunt ducks. After a long cold winter, he would say it was time to go fishing when the leaves on the trees were the size of a mouse's ear. Now I thought that was the funniest thing I'd heard in a long time. Then I got to thinking that I really don't know how big a mouse ear is supposed to be cause I've never seen one. I think those little critters are in Mr. P and LB's field of expertise. Well, LB's anyway cause I don't think ol' fluffy boy would move fast enough to actually catch one. LB must be doing a good job of mouse patrol, too, cause like I said, I've never seen one.

Gotta go and remember—don't go fishin' till the tree leaves are just the right size.

Kodi

Herding Cats

Hi Y'all,

Hope all is well at your ranch. I've been rather busy helping work cattle with babies, and I've decided that separating baby calves from their mamas is like trying to herd unruly cats. I had to help pen some mamas and babies so the little ones could get ear tags and all their shots. As long as I was just pushing them up to and into the pens, all was fine, but when we got them separated into different pens, the bellowing and bawling was so loud, I could hardly hear myself bark. I kept trying to tell my girls just to chill out. I mean their babies were right next to them for Pete's sake, but they didn't appreciate my comments at all. And since I was the smallest thing around, I got most of their verbal abuse. *Mooooo* took on some different meanings that I probably shouldn't repeat. Finally, the task was complete, and the mamas and babies got back together. Whew, what a morning!

I was one tired pup when we got back to the house and decided a little snooze in the cool grass under the pecan tree was in order. I got my belly all stretched out and was just dozing off when I heard a bird squawking at me. Seems she had her nest in that tree and was none too happy with me being there. I thought, *Not another crazy mama*. She squawked and squawked and even flew down and poked my wiggly butt with her sharp beak. That annoyed me to say the least, and I thought if she would get down on the ground, I might just eliminate her and her bad attitude.

I was tired and not in the mood to put up with her. I kept wondering why my being there bothered her so much cause I'm not a cat and can't climb trees. Go bother Mr. P or LB. LB might actually be a threat to her babies, but not me unless they just happen to fall on the ground, and then I might lick on them some since I do have trouble holding my licker. Finally, Mama came out and got me cleaned up, and I headed into the house. I hope those baby birds grow and learn to fly real soon cause I just know Mrs. Mockingbird is going to be difficult to live with till then.

So long from a tired little working dog,

Kodi

Blaaaaaah

Hi Y'all,

Well, the heat of a Texas summer is in full swing. It's sure been hot and dry in this part of the state. I have a feeling I'll be staying in the house as much as possible where the AC is. That cool tile floor calls my name a lot when the weather's like this.

I've been on the road a lot as of late. Sometimes I don't know where I'm going to lay my head from week to week. Course I love to travel and meet new folks, so don't think I'm complaining. I know lots of pups aren't as lucky as me.

Recently we were visiting a ranch out west of here, looking at some bulls, and I met up with a new critter called a goat. These folks raise them along with cattle, and there were hundreds of the red-headed things. It was the time of the year for them to have their babies, and they all seemed to have two or three. Mama and Daddy said they were so cute that we ought to bring a couple of the little ones home with us. My first thought was I'd have to share the back seat of the truck with two crying kids cause that's what they're called. And I would have to learn their language and everything. I know how to speak *moooooo* but not *blaaaah*. The crisis was adverted though since they don't stay cute for very long and then they start to look like—you guessed it—goats.

I agree the babies are kind of cute in their own way but grown ones, not so much.

From there, we headed to Abilene for the Western Heritage weekend. We went there last year, and I really enjoyed the outing. Lots of folks have their dogs with them, so I got to meet and greet lots of other canines. That night, my folks went to the Ranch Rodeo, but I stayed in the hotel room. Since I was pretty tuckered out watching the inside of my eyelids, uh, the TV, while curled up in a comfy bed suited me just fine.

Not long after that, we headed to the mountains of northern New Mexico for some R&R in a cool place. One morning while out with my folks on a hike, I heard a barking sound coming from some holes in the ground. I investigated but saw nothing. The next day, I heard the same sound, but this time one of the little critters was above ground, and I took off after him. Mama said I looked like a cutting horse the way I was keeping him from getting back to his hole. At one point, I actually caught the furry little thing, but I let go cause I didn't know what to do with him. He took off, and I resumed my chase, but there was dust and fur flying everywhere. The rest of his group must have sent out signals every time they saw me comingcause I never saw any more prairie dogs as they're called.

I don't know where the time has gone, but I turned two years old a while back. And I got that pretty new collar I was wishing for. It's bright red with shiny little dog bones all around. It really looks good on me too. I have a red bandana that I can wear with it as well. Course I'll wear my new stuff only when we're on a trip or at a cattle event. I'll keep my old one for every day and work. If you ask me, a girl can never have too many pretty things.

Well, guess I'd better sign off. I just heard my name called, and it's time to go and move my girls to another field to graze on some fresh grass for a few days. We're back on pretty good terms now. You may remember they got kind of mad at me when I had to separate them from their babies for a spell. Those good feelings will last till I have to make them do something they don't want to do. Oh well, that's the life of a little cowdog.

Happy trails to ya,

Kodi

Happy Birthday USA

Hi Y'all,

How's it going at your place? Sure is hot and dry here in my part of the world. That means we're spending lots of time moving my girls from pasture to pasture to graze. I think they'll be as glad as me when cooler weather arrives. Soon it'll be time to wean calves, and it'll sound like a feed lot around here since the weaning pens are close to the house. There'll be lots of bawling and bellowing from the calves as well as their mamas. They know I help separate them from their babies, so I'll get some dirty looks each time we go for our daily check of things. But after a week or so, things will quieten back down, and that'll make Mr. P happy since all that racket disturbs his twenty-three-hour naps.

Since my last letter, the USA celebrated a birthday on the Fourth of July. My folks went to an air show, but I had to stay home cause dogs weren't allowed. Don't know why, but sometimes that's just the way it is. Mama said I wouldn't have had much fun anyway cause it was soooooooo hot. So I'm glad I was at home in the AC where it was cool. Later on, we went to a fireworks display at a nearby lake, and that was like nothing I'd ever seen before. I bet my eyes were big as saucers with all the booms and crackles and noise. We sat in the back of the truck and had a real good view of all the explosions. Mama was afraid I might be scared of all the commotion since it was real loud, but since I've been getting so much verbal abuse from my girls lately, a few booms were nothing.

Lately I've become concerned about something, and it's my obsession with chasing LB. You know she and I are not the best of buds like me and Mr. P. And my chasing her every chance I get my have something to do with that. But lately, I can't seem to think of anything else when I see her. When she's at the house, she often hangs out above the deck, and she will lie there with her tail or foot hanging down when she knows I can't get to her. It's like she's saying, "Na na na na, you can't get me." It drives me crazy, and I think she knows it. I even run to the barn in a mad dash just to see if she's out there on top of a hay roll every time I go outside. The whole thing has me worried, and I sure hope I don't have to see a doggie psychiatrist about this addiction.

So long and I'll keep you posted on my "little" problem.

Kodi

Those Rascals

Hi Y'all,

Man, but I'm gettin' tired of this hot, dry weather. At least summer's half over, and soon we'll be enjoying the cool days of fall. We finally got a little rain last week, but it'll take a lot more to make much of a difference in this drought. It's so dry that the grasshoppers have invaded the yard and are eating on the shrubbery around our house. Mama said she'd never seen that before. Those things are kind of fun to chase though. They jump every which way, and so do I. Anyone looking out the window at me probably thinks I've gone a little nuts in the heat, but you have to act a bit crazy to catch one of those pesky bugs. They do come by their name naturally.

Because of the drought, we've been weaning calves a little earlier than usual so their mamas won't need quite as much grass to eat to stay in shape. Once those young'uns get through with their bawling, I think they forget about their moms pretty quickly cause they can be in adjoining pastures and act like they've never known each other. I guess that's nature's way. I wonder if I'd know my brothers and sisters if I were to meet up with them after all this time. Probably not.

We just got back from a wedding up in Arkansas. Course I stayed back in the hotel room during the event itself, but I got to go to the preparty since it was at the ranch the groom manages. That sure was a fun time.

The afternoon of the party, Mama and I were out walking when I spied some critters I'd never seen before. They were waddling along quacking as they headed to a big pond. I took off after them, but they were too fast for me. And since swimming was kind of a new thing to me, I decided not to get too far from the bank. Mama said they were Canadian geese, and they sure were bigger than the ducks we have on our ponds at home. When I got out of the water, I decided I needed a good run. I took off and ran and ran and buzzed around Mama till I was pooped. I plopped down next to her, and she was laughing like crazy. Seems like my running makes her happy, but since it was hot, all that activity took the zing out of me. I sat there for a spell, and then we headed to the horse barn to cool down. It was air-conditioned and oh so nice and cool. I was glad to chill out there the rest of the evening.

When we got home, something happened the very next morning. I woke up just as the sun was rising and just felt like something was amiss. When my folks got up shortly thereafter and let me out, I knew what was wrong cause a group of yearling bulls were in the yard, not in the pasture where they were supposed to be. They must have been there for a while too cause they had managed to make a mess. I started my bark that meant something was wrong and Mama and Daddy came running. Boy, she was not happy when she saw overturned flowerpots and stomped-on grass. She called those rascals some things I probably shouldn't repeat either. With my herding skills and knowledge of their language, we got them back to where they belonged. Then my folks started cleaning up things, and Daddy got the fence repaired where they got out. I learned when I was a little tyke that Mama takes pride in the yard and flowers looking just so, and it took her a lot of time and sweat to get things back in order. I thought to myself that those boys had better stay put, or they might find themselves on someone's hamburger.

Stay cool and think rain,

Kodi

The Alien

Hi Y'all,

Well, we're still waiting on rain and cooler weather around here, and it can't come soon enough for me. You know I don't like it hot especially when I have cattle work to be done, and that's just what I had to do the other day. Man, was I a pooped pup afterwards. The whole thing started when Daddy and I were out checking on my girls and their babes in different pastures. We came upon one group, and their babies were nowhere to be seen. My girls didn't seem too concerned at the time, but probably would have been pretty soon. Daddy noticed there was a break in the fence that separated that field from a wooded area. That must have been where they made their escape. We headed out on foot or paw, in my case, through the thicket and saw the rascals and started roundin' them up so we could push them back through that spot in the fence. All was okie-dokie till one—there's always one— decided he didn't want to go through that break and headed in the other direction, and the others followed him. It's always like herding cats when you have to fool with young calves. We worked and worked getting those young'uns back to where they were supposed to be, and finally I had to get downright rude. I let them know if they didn't get through that break in the fence right now, things were going to get ugly. Since I speak their language, they finally understood the consequences of not doing what I said.

It was hot, and Daddy and I were tuckered out by then, so we headed back to the house for a cool drink and a rest under the shade tree out back. Cattle work can be very tiring sometimes, but I guess when you're a little cowdog, it comes with the territory.

The next day, I was rested and full of vim and vigor. We got in our morning walk, and as usual, I was kind of dirty, so Mama rinsed me off and left me outside to dry. I decided I'd better make a check of things since we'd been gone for over an hour. Well, on my second trip around the house, I spied something very strange. It was under a shrub, had a hard back, but no head nor legs that I could see. Then I recalled something on TV about aliens and their flying saucers, so I got to thinking could this be one of them. It looked kind of the same as what I'd seen. I decided to investigate further by poking it with my paw. Nothing happened, no movement, nothing. So I poked it again and still nothing. Finally, I decided that barking might get some reaction, so I tried that. Now I have several barks in my wheelhouse, but the one I was using meant something was wrong. The alien didn't move, but Mama did come out to see what I was making such a fuss about. I ran over to where the thing was, expecting her to get all excited, but she just shook her head and told me to leave it alone cause it was just a big ol' turtle. What the heck is a turtle?

Anyway, I guess we were safe cause she went back in the house and came back in a few minutes and picked the alien up and carried it down to the pond north of the house. She told me that's where they live. Well, if that's true, then how did it get so far from its home without any legs? I'm still not convinced that it was a turtle and not some alien in a turtle suit. The TV show did say they could transform themselves into all sorts of things.

So long for now. Be wary of things that may not be what they seem to be. Just saying.

Kodi

Ol' Meathead

Hi Y'all,

If you ask me, this weather is stuck in a rut, which is hot and dry. I'm only two years old, but I got to thinking that I haven't seen much rain since I came here to live. Now we did have some snow my first two winters, and was that ever fun to play in. I'd really enjoy getting wet sometime other than when I get a bath. I can just see myself lying in the cool grass as some raindrops fall on my head. That would sure feel good. I guess it'll happen eventually, and the days will get cooler, but not soon enough for me.

I had a strange experience the other morning. I was out running in the pasture with my folks nearby when I spotted a big black bird. As I got closer, I recognized it to be a buzzard or Texas turkey. I speeded up some and got ready to give chase and make him fly. I ran and barked, but he just hippity-hopped and flippity-flopped his wings but stayed on the ground. He even ran into a gate and then a fence. I kept following right on his tail feathers all through the hay meadow with him flopping and hopping along. Finally after a bit, he stopped and turned around and said, "Kid, I'm tired of this game you're playing, so say we call it quits? My name's Meathead, and yours is?"

"Kodi," I replied.

"Oh, I've heard of you. You're the little cowdog around these parts. I think you met my two boys, Herkel and Jerkel, a while back when they were enjoying the aroma of piles of chicken litter."

I said I remembered them but didn't mention that I thought they weren't the handsomest of critters. "Why aren't you flying like other buzzards do? I mean I've been chasing you for a while now."

"Well, kid, that's kind of an embarrassing story. You see my eyesight's not what it used to be, and the other day, I sort of missed my landing in that dead tree over there and flew into it headfirst. I gave myself a concussion and messed up my left wing. And I still have a headache, so your barking is not helping at all. My banged-up left wing sort of has me grounded for a spell, so no flying right now."

I told him I was sorry for his accident and wouldn't bother him again and hoped he'd be better soon. He thanked me and moseyed off, so I headed back to my folks who were walking on the pasture road. Chasing an ol' crippled buzzard with bad eyesight is no fun, so I looked around for something else that might need chasing. Didn't find anything, so I just had a good run anyway cause sometimes a pup's just gotta go for it.

Gotta run,

Kodi

Pack Up and Let's Go

Hi Y'all,

It's finally September, and fall is just around the corner—YEAH! This sure has been a hard summer on anything that lives outdoors, what with the hot temperatures and little to no rain. I'm sure one lucky pup since I get to live indoors with the AC.

Since I'm head of security around here, not much bothers me except for gondolas and helicopters, so what I'm about to tell you I hope you'll keep to yourself. We went to a bull riding event this past weekend and stayed at a hotel we'd stayed at before. But this time, things were different cause there was a big fair going on in the parking lot next to the coliseum. Well, for some reason, all those lights, Ferris wheels, flopping flags, rollercoasters, etc. scared me so much that I didn't even want to go for walks. I was a nervous wreck the whole time we were there. As long as I was in our room, all was okay, but let me have to go outdoors and see all that commotion and my heart would get to racing like crazy. Wonder why that bothered me so. I mean I work cattle, and that can be dangerous at times, but being scared of all this has me baffled. I sure was glad when we loaded up and headed home. I slept like a baby most of the way. I guess stress can make you extra tired. Now I sure don't want my girls to hear about this cause I have a reputation to uphold and can't have this getting around. If they thought I was a scaredy cat, then the next time I told them to get moving or face the consequences, they'd probably just look at me and laugh. So let's just keep this incident between us, okay?

Speaking of being afraid, there are some things that being afraid of is a smart thing to do, and that's all the wildfires that have been happening here in Texas. Since we've been in a terrible drought for months now, the trees and grass are dry as a bone, and a tiny spark of fire could cause a big inferno. Luckily, we haven't had any fires near our ranch, but we've smelled the smoke from some close by. Lots of folks have had to evacuate their homes in a hurry, and I got to thinking about what I would take if we had to pack and go. Of course I'd definitely want my food and water and my pretty red collar that looks so good on me. Then there's my Kong toy that Mama fills with peanut butter. There's my squeaky toy and my stuffed bear that I like to sleep with cause that would give me some comfort during a stressful time. I definitely would grab my chewy bones and my rope toy to play with. I guess that would about do it. Hey, that's everything in my toy box. Hmmmmmm, it might be hard for me to make those tough choices of what to take in a hurry.

Well, so long for now and pray for rain.

Kodi

OMG, I forgot about Mr. P. He would definitely be on my list of things to grab in a hurry. He would be easy to find too since I know all his napping spots. The main thing that would concern him would be that we take plenty of his food since he has to nibble all day long to keep up his strength, or so he says. I guess LB would have to fend for herself. She stays in the big hay barn most of the time, and she wouldn't believe me anyway if I told her she needed to come down and get ready to leave. She'd just think I was trying to trick her so I could give her a good chase. She's pretty scrappy, so I'm sure she'd be okay in an emergency. Hopefully it won't come to that.

The Pecan Snatcher

Hi Y'all,

You know a while back I was worried I might need to see a doggie psychiatrist about my obsession with chasing LB? Well, that's the least of my worries now cause we've been invaded by a beady-eyed, fluffy-tailed pecan snatcher. I've been trying to tell my folks with my special bark that something was in that tree out back, but they just thought I was being obsessive about LB when they knew she was at the barn. But yesterday, the proof came down from that tree and ran right in front of me. Now I'll admit I was kind of in snoozy land since I'd been busy with cow work and was tired, but when that little blur ran in front of my sleepy eyes and jumped into another tree, I came to my senses in a flash. I was hot on its fluffy tail in 1.2 seconds. And yes, it was a squirrel and right in my back yard nonetheless. Now with the drought, pecans will be in short supply, and I don't want to share any of those delicious nuts with a pesky squirrel. Of course I can't be on pecan tree guard duty all the time since I have other things to do, so I'm sure that thing will get some, but what really bothers me is if a squirrel can invade my turf so easily, then what other critters do I have to worry about?

Several months ago, we took Misty, Sug's daughter, to a kind of horse boarding school so she could begin her education under saddle. Well, this past week, we went and picked her up to come home for a while and have a break from her training schedule. You know, kind of like horse R&R. Back when we dropped her off, I met one of the trainers' dogs, and we had a lot of fun playing and chasing each other. This time, I met the other dog and first thought something was wrong with her face. I asked if she had run into a brick wall or something cause it was all smashed in. She laughed and said, "No, silly pup, that's just how I look; I'm a French bulldog."

I'd never met one before, so if they're supposed to look that way, so be it. We got along just fine, and we ran and played, but it was hot and we ran out of steam pretty quickly. She kept complaining how the heat was harder on her since she had that smashed-in face, so I thought then, *"Why don't you chill out a little?*

She seemed a little hyper, and that's saying a lot coming from yours truly. And I bet she snored when she slept too cause she made funny sounds when she was panting. Eventually it was time for us to head out, so I said goodbye and got in the cool truck. When we pulled into the barn area at home, Sug came a-running. And when Misty got unloaded and joined her, they took off in a flash with their tails up high running and having a grand ol' time. My folks kept saying how pretty Misty was since her coat was the color of a new shiny penny. She'd been in a stall a lot so her coat didn't have a chance to get sunburned in the hot Texas sun. It was good to have her home for a spell and see her out in the pasture again.

So long for now. I'm headed out for pecan tree duty. I mean someone's got to keep those pesky things at bay.

Kodi

Tattoos

Hi Y'all,

Guess what? It finally rained here at our ranch! Not a gully washer mind you, but more than we've had in a very long time, so every drop was welcomed. There were puddles everywhere, and I had a grand time running and jumping into every one I came across. I got all wet and dirty and knew a bath was coming my way, but what the heck, I thought.

The other afternoon, I was out patrolling near the big hay barn, checking for intruders when I realized I hadn't talked to anyone all day. I looked around to see who I could strike up a conversation with and noticed all my girls were out grazing and the young bulls were resting in the shade of some trees, but then I spotted Sug. She and Misty were by the gate waiting for Mama to come out and give them an apple treat; they love those things as much as I do peanut butter and popcorn. Well, it was about then I noticed Sug had a tattoo on her right hip in the shape of a backward 7. I'm sure it's been there all along, but I just noticed it. I moseyed over and asked why she chose that particular tat. She looked down at me kind of puzzled like and said, "Wiggle Butt, that's not a tattoo. It's a scar I got when I was about Misty's age when I backed into some barbed wire."

I told her, "It sure looks like one, but if you say it's a scar, then that's what we'll call it." That got me to thinking that I'm the only thing around here, except for my folks, Misty, and LB, who doesn't have some kind of special marking. All my girls have them, and when their babies are weaned, then they get them too. Course they're called brands, but it's the same thing if you ask me. What kind should I get if my folks would let me have one? Maybe a western hat or a tiara since I'm pretty like a princess. But where would I put it? I'm covered in fur except for my tongue and inside my ears, and I don't think I would like someone poking holes in my licker. I guess I'll put that on my list of things that will never happen cause I know my folks wouldn't let me have one anyway.

Sug and Misty wandered off, so I headed over to one of Mr. P's napping spots to get his opinion on the subject of tats. I pounced on him, and he sort of woke up with one eye half open. "What do you want?" he asked.

"Hey, what kind of tattoo should I get, and where would I put it?"

"You woke me up to ask me a silly question like that? Go away and bother someone else."

Actually he doesn't know it, but he has a tattoo of sorts by the way his hair lies on his forehead. He's a breed of cat called a Maine coon, and they're all big and fluffy like him, and he has an *M* on his forehead formed by some dark hairs. I think that's neat, don't you? I'm a little Aussie, but I don't have an *A* on my forehead. If I did, then that would be my tattoo.

Guess I'd better go. I'm sure something needs my attention. Hey, I need to find LB and see what she thinks of my getting a tat. She'll probably tell me she'll give me one with her claws if I don't quit chasing her so much. Actually I think she likes it but would never admit it to me.

Kodi

Quacked up

Hi Y'all,

Hope all is well at your place. Things are finally looking green around here since we've had more rain in the last three weeks than we had all summer. Course now it's time for a frost since the temps are gettin' lots colder, but the green sure is nice for a short time anyway. Since chilly weather is finally here, there are changes in critters' behavior as well. Mr. P must think a hard winter is coming since he's really been putting away the vittles. He actually lost some weight this past miserably hot summer, but he's making up for lost time now. Daddy says he almost needs a back brace to pick up the big guy. Course P maintains he's not getting fat, just a little fluffier. I'm thinking the scales at our vet clinic tell a different story.

The other morning, I was out patrolling my territory when I heard a noise I'd never heard before. My folks were outside too, looked up, and excitedly said that geese were flying overhead headed south for the winter. I looked up and saw a big bunch of birds flying in a *V* formation, quacking for all they were worth. It seems that they leave their home up north when it gets real cold and head south, kind of like some people do. I kept thinking that sure was a long way to travel just by flapping wings the whole way. I mean I have lots of energy, but that would tire even me out.

Mama asked Daddy if he remembered one chilly foggy morning when a group of snow geese landed in the pasture north of the house to rest till the fog lifted so they could navigate better. I guess they didn't want to quack up. Get it? Quack up. Oh, well, she said they stayed for over an hour and then flew away. Isn't it neat how all critters know just what to do to survive all kinds of weather? I know what to do when it's too hot or too cold—I go inside, and that sounds like a good idea right about now since a little nap is in my future plans.

So long and I'll let you know about Mr. P's weight situation.

Kodi

The Mystery of the Messed-Up Bed

Hi Y'all,

Don't know about your place, but it's gotten rather cold around here. It was freezing this morning with a heavy frost on everything. That makes it look like it's snowed. After this past hot summer, these cold mornings make me extra frisky, and sometimes I get the urge to run, and I go and go till I drop. Then I'm ready for a nap, and that brings up some things that happen every so often. Usually I nap stretched out on the cool tile floor, but now that the weather's colder, I like to nap in a softer place. So when no one's looking, I head off to the guest bedroom and get the covers and throw pillows just to my liking and take a snooze. Now this usually happens when I'm in the house by myself. Course when Mama comes in and finds that bed messed up, I hear my named called. When she calls me in a certain way, I know I'm in trouble. I really don't know what the big deal is. No one's using that bed when I take a nap on it. But for some reason, she wants it to stay just so-so being a neat freak like I've learned she is.

Now I've never gotten into real trouble as I always manage to get off the bed before getting caught, but the evidence proves I've been there. That's going to stay my little secret too of how I manage to never be seen in that compromising position. Even Mr. P is amazed at how I've never been caught on it, and I'm not telling him either.

I had a new experience the other day. I got to ride on a float in a parade honoring veterans. It was quite an honor to get to do that. I hear everyone say we should always remember the men and women who fought and died for the freedoms we have in the good old USA. I was on my best behavior the whole time and would have waved at folks if I had hands instead of paws. There were lots of bands and twirlers and drill teams and horses, and from my viewpoint, everyone was having a grand time.

Remember to thank a veteran when you see one. I would give him/her a good face washing as my way of saying "thanks ". You know I can't hold my licker very well. I hope that would show them just how much I appreciate their service.

So long. I may just go do a little napping and you know where – he-he-he

Kodi

Happy, Merry, Happy

Hi Y'all,

I've decided to lump all my holiday greetings into this one letter, so here goes, "Happy Thanksgiving, Merry Christmas, Happy New Year!"

Seems these holidays are so close together that one greeting could do for all three. Wonder why these special days aren't spread out a little further so all this good cheer could last longer?

I've been thinking of what to put on my Christmas wish list this year, and so far a new toy for my folks to throw for me to chase when we're outdoors is at the top. I'm getting real good at catching things in midair, but I've found that I have to pace myself some cause a game of that will tire you out pretty quickly. Since I tend to go through chewy toys so fast, I can always use an ample supply of those things. And I really do need a new stuffed toy to snooze with since most of mine have lost their stuffing and are more rags than toys.

I asked Mr. P what was on his list, and he said more peace and quiet. Wonder what he meant by that. I guess he may not want me pouncing on him so much when he's taking one of his looooonnnnnngggg naps. He's getting up in years, so he says he needs more rest, and I think he's getting plenty. If it weren't for me, he probably wouldn't get any exercise at all, so I'm doing him a favor by disturbing him all the time. I keep hearing on the news that we all need to be more active to stay healthy, so I'll go on pestering him every chance I get, and that way, he'll live a long time. You know how I love that big ol' furry guy.

Speaking of chewy toys, I often have a dilemma as to where to hide them, especially when I have leftovers. One of my favorite hiding places is behind the pillows on my folks' bed. That works out just fine till Mama notices the pillows out of order, and then I have to move my treasure. The couch pillows are good places for hiding as well, but again when those pillows are not in place, I hear my name called, and I know the drill. "Move this thing or lose it." If you have any ideas for safe hiding places, let me know. Maybe there needs to be a doggie bank for things like that and maybe even a doggie savings plan for chewies. Wonder if that might be a solution.

Well, time to go and find a hiding place for this morning's leftover chewy. Decisions, decisions.

Kodi

Santa Kodi

Hi Y'all,

Hope your Christmas was all you hoped for. We had a big gathering at our house this year, and I loved getting to see all my family, humans and dogs alike. So many faces to lick, butts to sniff, and so little time.

Now there was one downside to this year's festivities. I had to have my picture taken wearing a Santa outfit! Can you believe that? One of my folks' friends has a weird sense of humor and sent a Santa outfit for me to wear. I had a hat, beard, and things to wear around my ankles that had little bells on them. I can't believe I had to wear that getup and then, to add to my humiliation, have my picture taken. Now every Christmas, I'll think of that. I sure was glad I didn't have to go outside and be seen by my girls cause they would have laughed me out of the pasture. But Mr. P and LB did see me, and he had a smirky grin on his face. I could tell he was trying to keep from giggling, and if he had, I might just have had to pounce on him real hard. He told me later that no self-respecting cat would ever submit to wearing something like that. I told him I didn't actually have a choice in the matter. I mean I'm a working cowdog and head of security, not some Santa impersonator. I'm sure glad no one else saw me; oh wait—there's a picture. Jeez Louise. I bet my folks will e-mail that to all their friends, and they'll get a good laugh. Hopefully I won't have to wear some bunny outfit at Easter.

You know I think I came across another alien the other day. We were on a pasture walk, and I was ahead of my folks when I spotted a big rubberlike thing with a long tail hanging off it. It was just lying there in the grass, and I know it wasn't there the day before. I decided to investigate and make sure things were okay before my folks got too close. I mean the motto of us ranch dogs is safety first when it comes to our family. I crept closer and closer, but there was no movement, no sound, nothing. I circled it several times and gave it a good sniffing and then barked at it. Still nothing. Then I poked it with my paw, and all of a sudden, that thing exploded right in front of my eyes. The only thing left was its tail, and it kind of floated off into the air. I mean it just vanished.

This alien stuff has me baffled. Why are they coming here, and for what reason? Are they checking to see what life is like on a Texas ranch? I'd ask Mr. P his opinion, but he's yet to see one, so he'd just think I was talking crazy. You know he's in one place for long periods of time, so it sure would be easy for one of their ships to beam him up to study why he takes such long naps. Anyway I'm going to be on the lookout for any strange things I spot, and I'll keep you informed. And if you see or hear anything about alien sightings, be sure and let me know too.

Well, so long. Stay vigilant my friend as we never know who or what might be watching us from afar.

Kodi

Life's Good

HI Y'all,

Hard to believe we're already into a new year. Seems like just yesterday we were complaining about the heat, and now it's the middle of winter. And things are kind of strange too as my girls are out grazing grass more than they're eating hay. For some reason, grass is growing better than it did last summer. I guess since we've had some good rains that accounts for it. Or maybe the seasons are mixed up. There have been some aliens around, and I'm wondering if they could have a hand in this weird weather. Hmmmm.

A few days ago, I was out running in the pasture and was way ahead of my folks when I spotted a critter I'd not ever seen. I ran in its directions to get a better view. I could tell it sort of looked like one of my kind but had long legs. I started barking to indicate it had better have a good reason for being in my territory without my permission. But my barks didn't make it move at all. Then my folks caught up with me to see what all the ruckus was about, and Mama said the critter was a coyote. They're wild, and come to find out they're what makes all the howling and yipping noises at night. Mama said they can make enough noise to make you think there's a bunch of them when there'll only be two or three. And she said for me not to go chasing after any either since they could be dangerous. I thought then they'd better stay out of my territory, but I also decided that chasing after a wild critter might not be in my best interest, so I'll let them be. About then, it saw my folks and took off in the opposite direction from where we were.

Later on that evening, I got to thinking about how I'm sure living the good life. Here I was all comfy, cozy in my favorite chair with my stuffed bear by my side and ready for a nap. It just doesn't get much better than this unless I also had my Kong toy filled with peanut butter to lick out. I love that stuff as much as popcorn. Sorry but I got sidetracked with thoughts of that wonderful stuff. Anyway, I thought, man, I'm a lucky pup. I have a nice home to live in, folks who love and care for me. Actually I've got them wrapped around my paws if you know what I mean. I get to travel and have all kinds of adventures and meet new people and their dogs. I have lots of toys and a best bud to curl up with when he's in the mood. I know he's a cat, and we're supposed to be enemies like me and LB, but you couldn't ask for a better friend than that ol' cat. And I get to do what I was bred for, work cattle, so who could ask for more? I just wanted you to know how appreciative I am of my good fortune.

The downside to this day was that one of my girls had twin calves, and neither survived. Now and then, it just happens no matter how well my folks take care of my girls. The mama is doing okay and will bounce back soon, but I know she misses having those two little ones to care for. I didn't mean to be a downer, but this business is not always rosy. Sometimes sad things happen, and we have to put them behind us and keep on keeping on.

Guess I'd better sign off. It's been kind of rainy lately and seems like there are some puddles with my name on them. I'll get dirty and have to have a good cleaning before I can come inside and nap in that chair, but it'll be worth it.

Kodi

Bird Brained

Hi Y'all,

I heard that yesterday was Groundhog Day, and according to that furry little varmint, we're supposed to have six more weeks of winter weather since he saw his shadow. What's up with that? I see my shadow all the time, but it doesn't mean anything. I wonder if we have any varmits here in Texas that can predict the weather. Maybe George the Gopher, who knows? And if you ask me, the weather doesn't know that it's February cause it feels more like April. Wonder if we'll have snow in July.

Speaking of warmer weather, the crazy red birds are back! Our house has storm windows, and you can see your reflection in them. Many a time, I've strolled by and wondered who that cute face belonged to and then realized it was yours truly. Now if I've got this reflection stuff figured out, then why can't those goofy birds do the same? They take the expression *bird brained* to a whole new level. The red ones are kind of aggressive by nature. They may be pretty and all, but they have a fighting side when it comes to what they think is their territory. And when they see themselves in those windows, they go to war. They will peck and peck and peck at those windows for hours. Now wouldn't you think that after a bit, they would realize they're pecking at themselves, but noooooooo, they just keep on keeping on. It drives me bonkers when I'm indoors. I can be on the other side of a window barking my head off, and they act like I'm not even there. I woke Mr. P up to see if he would go take care of the problem if you get my drift, but he said they weren't bothering him and dozed back off. I thought birds were in a cat's field of expertise like mice, but I guess he didn't get that memo. Anyway this pecking ritual will go on for several weeks, and then they'll build their nests and get on with raising their batch of little bird-brained kids. Till then, I guess I'll just have to put up with it.

And another thing, have you ever heard a donkey braying? What a sound they can make and loud too! There's one in a neighboring pasture, and I can hear him from a long way off when he's gets to "talking." Now lots of folks think donkeys are cute, but I think maybe that's an acquired taste. And have you seen their ears? I bet they can pick up signals from outer space with those long things. Hey, maybe I need to make friends with Mr. Donkey-in-the-Next-Field and tell him to signal me with one long bray if he hears any aliens coming in for a landing. That one long bray could be our secret signal that only he and I knew about. I think the next time I see him near the fence, I'll mosey over and mention my idea and see what he thinks. I can't be on guard duty 24/7, so he might just come in handy as something other than a pasture pet.

Oh, I just heard him "talkin'," so I think I'll head over and make friends. I'll stay on my side of the fence though till I see if he likes little cowdogs or not. Better safe than sorry. If our meeting goes well, I'll tell you about it later.

Kodi

A Mad Mama Jamma

Hi Y'all,

It's sure nice to be able to say that all's good in the cattle business right now. Ponds are full, winter grass is lush, and my girls are happy as pigs in sunshine. Speaking of my girls, I came to the conclusion the other day that they can have a mob mentality. The day was going just great, and then it took a wrong turn. It was one of those winter days here in Texas that makes you want to be outside 'cause the sun was shining and there was a clear blue sky with a soft breeze blowing, you know that kind of day. Mama and I decided to go for a walk down through the pasture while Daddy decided to have a cup of coffee on the deck and read the paper. Mama walked and I ran and played till we noticed the cows in that pasture were following us. We were crossing a narrow pond dam when suddenly the entire herd came stampeding toward us. They were jumping and kicking and slipping and sliding. Mama stopped and yelled at them to stop before they ran us over. They all had a wild-eyed look on their faces, so we got to one side and let them all pass. They came running and headed off to another field like the devil was behind them with a whip. I thought 'how silly, the grass over there's no different than where they'd just been'. Mama and I decided to head back to the house, and when she mentioned the incident to Daddy, he asked if that new baby calf was with them. She said he wasn't in the bunch so we loaded up in the mule and went to find him cause he was just a few days old. The mob was two fields over by this time, and we found the little fellow asleep by the big pond. We drove up close so my folks could get him and carry him to his mama. That's where things took a nasty turn. He might have been little, but fought like a tiger when Daddy tried to put him in the mule. I guess his mama had told him to stay put, and he was trying to do just that, but we didn't want him all by hisself. He was kicking and bawling and Daddy was trying to get him to cooperate but with difficulty.

About this time, I looked up from this fracas and noticed his mama on the other side of that pond, and she was not a happy camper. She jumped into the water and came across headed in our direction. She was fighting mad to say the least. Oh, tell PETA that no animals were harmed during this incident, just people. Daddy got the little guy in the back of the mule and told Mama to "DRIVE!" and off we went with the mad mama cow trying to get in the front seat where yours truly was. I was being very quiet and still cause I didn't want her to remember that I had any part in this the next time I was in the vicinity of her back heels. Finally, we got that calf to where the rest of the herd was and put him out with his angry mother, and off they went. Whew what a ride! By then Daddy's clothes were, well, let's just say he couldn't ride up front with us or go into the house till he stripped down to his skivvies. And he was limping since that baby calf had kicked him all over. Mama was limping too cause she'd stepped in a hole trying to help. I was the only one not covered in mud and muck. How can such a perfect afternoon go so wrong so quickly? Some days it just doesn't pay to take a walk in the sunshine.

A thought to leave you with: sleeping calves are best left alone when their mamas are close by.

Kodi

A Sticky Situation

Hi Y'all,

How are things at your place? Hope all is as good as it is here. You know I'm a little cowdog, and I'm around cattle folks all the time. Lately I've noticed there's a difference between cow people and horse people and the kind of trailers they pull around and how their horses look in those trailers. Now my folks are in the cow people category even though we have two horses, namely, Sug and Misty. Mama used to show horses when she was younger, so I guess she fell into the horse people category then. Actually lots of cow folks have horses and use them for all sorts of jobs like driving cows from one place to another, separating and penning, you know, things like that. And when you see those horses, they're usually already saddled, loaded into a trailer, and ready for work. But I've noticed when you see horse people's horses, they usually have blankets on and are riding in fancy trailers with living quarters up front. They are most likely headed to a show or a cutting/roping/penning event. And they always look like they've just been groomed. Maybe this is not always the case, but it's just an observation from this little dog.

And I really noticed this difference the other day when we were at a cattle event. The hotel where we were staying was next to a big coliseum where lots of horse competitions are held. When Mama and I were out walking around, I kept noticing all the fancy trailers that pulled into the parking lot. Each one seemed nicer than the one before. Later on,

I got to noticing cattle trailers at our event, and they were nice. I mean my folks have a real nice one they pull cattle in, but nothing like those horse trailers. I guess cattle folk make a living from the cattle they haul around and horse folk are just there for fun.

Our event was being held at a ranch, and while there, I discovered something called cactus. Sure glad we don't have that stuff at our place as it can pose a big problem for a pup's paws! I guess if you live around it, you get used to pulling out those thorns or maybe have some custom doggie boots. I was out running around and managed to get some stuck in my right front paw. Mama noticed and came to my rescue since it stopped me in my tracks. And wouldn't you know it, a short time later, I got some more stuck in there. Finally, I learned to steer clear of that prickly stuff. I heard Mama say too that I shouldn't go poking my nose into any or I might just get a snake bite. Remember the time I got stung and my head swelled up for two days? Well, I bet a snake bite would be lots worse.

I heard someone say it isn't a good idea to squat with your spurs on, whatever that means. Well, if that's true, then it's probably not a good idea to squat in a field of cactus either. Just saying.

Kodi

Being Helpful

Hi Y'all,

Well, it's calving season around this ranch, and we've got lots of new babies being born. I love those newbies, especially when they get a few weeks old and their mamas don't freak out so much when I try to play with them. I like to dart around and get them running and jumping and just loving life. That usually doesn't last too long though cause when their mamas see who's causing all the ruckus, I get some verbal *moooo*s coming my way.

And speaking of calves, I had to earn my keep, as they say, the other morning. I decided that some days, it just doesn't pay to try and be helpful. I helped separate the babies from their mamas so Daddy could put in their ear tags and thought I might as well get out of the way for a bit. I headed to the mule for a little nap since it was one of those days with warm sunshine and a cool breeze and my eyelids had gotten kind of heavy. I guess I was dreaming of stampeding cattle when I awoke suddenly and all my girls and their babies were headed in my direction! I jumped out of the mule and started barking to get them to go back the other direction, which they did and nearly ran over Daddy in the process. Whoops. Seems like he was trying to get them out of the corral, and in my sleepy stupor, I was putting them back just where he didn't want them. You guessed it—yes, I got some more verbal abuse of the human kind about then. "Kodi, get out of the way. Don't push them back on me. What are you thinking? You're supposed to be helping!"

My only thought was some days being helpful doesn't always go as planned.

On another note, I'm trying to decide whether the life of a beach bum or a snow bunny suits me better. Recently while at a cattle event, we took some time and drove down to a nearby beach for a few hours. I got to run and play in that sand and chase seagulls to my heart's content. Now the weather was a little warm for my taste cause you know I like it cool better. And my folks kept telling me not to drink any of the water that I was splashing around in, or it might make me sick. Now that was lots of fun, but I think I might be more suited to mountain life and when there's snow on the ground even better. In the summer, it's nice and cool there, and in the winter, there's snow to play in and that is *fun*. And I don't mean to poke fun, but have you ever seen humans trying to learn to ski?

There was a big window at the condo we stayed at, and I could see the beginner slopes, so while my folks were out on the mountain, I had great fun watching people fall and try to master the art of staying on those long boards strapped to their feet. I don't seem to fall when I'm out in it, but then I do have built-in four-wheel drive.

I got to thinking that either place might be hard on my girls. If they couldn't drink the water, then that wouldn't do, and lots of snow might not be to their liking either. I've noticed that when we've had snow here at home, they do seem to need more to eat to help stay warm. I really like being a little cowdog, so I imagine I'll be staying right where I belong, but it sure is fun to go to the beach or to the mountains for a visit from time to time.

Guess I'll sign off and maybe go pounce on Mr. P and see which he likes better, the beach or the mountains. Course I know the answer—"Anyplace that you're not right now." Love that ol' guy.

Kodi

Twins

Hi Y'all,

Man oh man, this weather we've been having lately sure is right up my alley. It's been cool and sunny, and a nice breeze has been blowing. After the storms we had last week, we deserve some pretty days. Actually the word *storm* might not be strong enough to describe what occurred. When I'm indoors, I don't mind thunder and lightning too much, but this time, I decided the best place for me was under the bed cause it was louder than usual. That's where I stayed too till Mama came and convinced me all was ok and I could come out. I've heard it said you should seek shelter when a bad storm hits, and that's what I did.

I think I forgot to mention in my last letter that one of my girls had twin baby heifers. My folks named them Itsy and Bitsy. Itsy is the smaller of the two, but she can jump and run and play just like the bigger calves. Actually she doesn't weigh much more than me right now, but soon she'll get to growing, and I won't be able to tell her from the rest of the calf mob. There's another calf out in that pasture who's become quite a pest. His name's Stormy cause of the weather the day he was born. He didn't know how to nurse or anything, so my folks spent a lot of time with him teaching him things like that. Now when he sees my folks, he comes and wants to be rubbed on his head. And he likes to butt ya too. That's cute now, but when he weighs 1,000 pounds, it won't be. Anyway it's great to see Itsy, Bitsy, and Stormy doing so well cause they all had a tough start in life.

I ran across some new critters this morning while out in the pasture. I was running way ahead of my folks when I spied a group of the ugliest things I'd seen lately. I don't mean to be rude, but the big ones were uuggllyy. There was a big bunch of them too. They were making grunting noises and rustling around in the grass. I stretched my neck as high as I could to get a better view and let them know from the look on my face that I wasn't very happy about them being in my territory without my permission. All of a sudden, they spotted me and took off in a hurry toward some nearby woods. I took off after them until one of the real big ones turned and headed back in my direction. I decided I might need to make a hasty retreat, and about that time, my folks saw what was happening and started yelling at the beast. He stopped in his tracks and headed back to his fleeing group. My folks said those ugly things were wild hogs and not to be messed with. They can be real dangerous and have long tusks that can rip you apart. I sure don't want to have to have any stitches so decided I would try to avoid any I came across again. I never know what kind of adventure I'll have each new day around this ranch.

By the way, have you ever had the pleasure of chewing on a horse hoof? You really don't know what you're missing if not. Sug and Misty got their hooves trimmed the other day, and there were pieces left over for me to enjoy. Now I have to keep my little treasures outside, so I hide them in different places, and then when I'm in the mood for some horse hoof chewing, I go and dig one up. The only problem is sometimes I kind of forget where I buried them and have to do some digging to find them. Mama really doesn't like me digging in her flowerbeds, so I have to be careful where I choose to hide them.

Gotta go. I need to go check on Itsy, Bitsy, and Stormy or avoid him if he's in a butting mood. Then I might just find one of those hoof pieces and do a little chewing. Don't knock it till you try it.

Kodi

Yip-Yip-Yippy-Ki-Oh

Hi Y'all,

Hope all is well at your place. We've had a few real chilly days around here lately, and Mama said that was probably our Easter spell. She says it's funny how ole weather sayings seem to hold true. And lately, the night sky has been so clear that you can see millions of twinkling stars when you look up. Mama said it made her feel like singing the song about the stars being big and bright deep in the heart of Texas. I'm kind of glad she didn't though cause truth be known she can't sing very well. In fact, I've noticed Daddy always turns up the radio volume some when we're in the truck so as to kind of drown out her humming.

Speaking of singing, the coyotes singing woke me up at daylight the other morning. It was one of those cold ones when you just want to stay curled up in your bed till the last possible moment. All of a sudden, it sounded like there was a pack right outside the bedroom window. They were yippin' and making all sorts of noise, and my folks were afraid they might be after Itsy or Bitsy. Daddy jumped out of bed in a flash, grabbed a gun, and went outside without even getting dressed to run them off. He got in a few shots at the two scoundrels as they headed for the hills in a hurry. The twins were okay, but it could have been serious if they had not been close to their mama.

Itsy, being such a little thing, wouldn't have had much of a chance against two grown coyotes. The biggest thing about her are those ears of hers. I told Mr. P the other day that I bet Itsy could fly if she could flap those things. He just about fell over laughing and said that calves can't fly. I told him I heard an expression about pigs flying, so if porkers with their little ears could go airborne, then why not Itsy? He just shook his head and said," You are such a silly pup."

Then I got to thinking more about pigs and the movie called *Babe*. Well, that porker learned the language that sheep speak and even learned to herd those wooly things. He learned that "ba-ram-you" meant "To the breed be true." So if that pig could learn a language and some can fly on occasion, then I don't see why Itsy couldn't do the same with her big ears a flapping. Wouldn't that be something to see? And I bet folks would come from everywhere to see a flying calf. She might even get her own reality show on tv called *The Flying Calf of Texas*. It would be about all her adventures and what she sees from flying over the countryside. I would be her sidekick of course, and since I'm already head of security, I could help protect her from all the paparazzi. Hey, it could happen.

A while back, we had some visitors from Down Under. Now I don't know why Australia is called that or what it's under, so I guess that's another question for Google. They had gotten in the Brangus business and were in the U.S. touring ranches. They were super nice folks and spoke the same language as Mama and Daddy does, but it sounded kind of different. Couldn't quite put a paw as to what the difference was though. We were in the Ranger going down a side road headed to the west pasture, and the man said that if we were in his country, we would be driving on the other side of the road. I thought that sounded kind of dangerous and wondered how they kept from running into other vehicles. And being from Australia, they knew all about us wiggly butts since some of my ancestors worked there on big sheep ranches. They did say that those little dogs aren't quite as groomed as I usually am and don't live in the house nor sleep with a stuffed bear. I guess I'm a real lucky pup to live the life I do.

Well, gotta go. Oh, if you see any UFCs flying overhead, let me know. That's short for "unidentified flying calves"—ha ha!

Kodi

Angry Birds

Hi Y'all,

Looks like warm weather is here for the next few months. Soon I'll be saying hot weather, but that's Texas for ya. For those of us who have lived in the Lone Star State for any length of time, we know it'll cool back down about October. Till then, I try to stretch out on the cool tile floor as much as possible. When I come inside to escape the heat, I get my little tummy on that cool floor and try to position myself right under a ceiling fan. That way, the tile cools my underside, and the fan cools my topside. Smart, huh?

These warm days have bought back the hummingbirds too. Mama hung some feeders around the deck out back so they can get plenty of that high-octane sugar water to drink. Seems they need to refuel themselves a lot since their little wings beat so fast that they use up lots of energy. They kind of remind me of jet fighter planes the way they fly around so fast here and there. And they sure don't like to share either. I mean there's plenty of that sugary stuff to go around, so I keep wondering why they fuss so much about having to share the same feeding station. I got to wondering the other day if Mr. P had ever caught one and then laughed at the idea of him moving that fast. I decided the only way fluffy boy would ever catch a hummer is if it flew into a wall, knocked itself out, and fell into his food bowl.

Unfortunately, the warmer weather has brought another bird back, and that's Mrs. Mockingbird. She likes to set up housekeeping in the pecan tree out back, and after she builds her next and her eggs hatch, she goes into "angry bird" mode. No one is safe from her. She'll fly down and try to poke my wiggly butt with that sharp beak of hers and dive-bombs me and anyone else that comes close. And her squawky voice gets on my nerves. I bet whoever designed that video game *Angry Birds* had an encounter with her on occasion. I'm always glad when her young'uns fly away so it's safe to be under that tree again.

We've been on the go some lately. There have been cattle events to attend and then one of my favorite outings, the Western Heritage weekend out in Abilene. I love walking around meeting new folks and their dogs, but one of my favorite things is getting to sample foods on a stick like corn dogs and cheese cake. Mama said she didn't know why food tasted so good when it was on a stick, and I agree. One of the highlights of the weekend is the matched horse races. I got to thinking that matched dog races might be a good draw too. Now I wouldn't want to run as far as the horses do, but a race would be fun. And since I can put the *run* in *running*, I would definitely bet on myself to win.

When we get home from any trip, long or short, I always make a beeline for the big hay barn. LB needs to know that I'm back and ready for a good chase. I mean she might have missed me. Probably not though. And of course I have to go find Mr. P and pounce on him just to hear him say, "Go away, little dog. You're bothering me." It never gets old.

Well, it's a little too warm out, and the cool tile is calling my name, so a short nap sounds like a good idea. I can doze peacefully knowing that the angry bird can't bother me in here.

Kodi

One, Two, Three

All together now: "Happy birthday to you! Happy birthday to you! Happy birthday, sweet Kodi! Happy birthday to you. And many more!"

You sounded great. I can't believe I've just turned three years old. I guess time really does fly when you're having fun. Seems like just yesterday I was just a wiggly ball of fur on my way to Texas. And now I've learned the language of *mooooo* and get to help with cattle work, which is what I was born to do. I have a good friend in the form of a fluffy cat, and I think he feels the same about me, most of the time. I get to travel, ride in a golf cart, live in the house, and have lots of toys and treats. *Hey life is good!* I know people get a cake on their special day with candles to blow out, but I got peanut butter in my Kong and some popcorn that night while TV watching. What a great day.

I wonder if my brothers and sisters are living large like me? If I could, I'd do a Google search and maybe find some of them. Or I could go on Facebook or Twitter. It would be fun to compare lives cause I think I hit the jackpot when it comes to my family.

Well, so long. Since I'm an adult now and not a crazy wild pup, I probably need to go do something productive. Course it is my birthday, so a nap wouldn't hurt, and it's nice outside, and Mrs. Mockingbird has left, so the shade of the pecan tree might just be a good place for a short snooze. That'll help me be more energized for tomorrow cause when you're a little cowdog, you never know what kinds of adventures are around the corner.

Happy trails to ya,

Kodi

Travels

Hi Y'all,

Since my birthday, we've been on the go some. We like to go to the mountains every chance we get and went to Angel Fire, New Mexico, for a few days to get away from the Texas heat. We stayed at the same hotel as before, and I was in a hurry to get out and check and see if those prairie dogs were still all around the parking lots. They were still there, but I didn't catch one this time. I sure tried, but they must have remembered me and sent up signals when they saw me coming cause every time I got near, they all made a quick dive into their holes. I stuck my nose in as far as I could but couldn't see anything in the dark. Mama said I was going to draw back a nub, but all I got was a dirty nose.

While there, we spent some time at another resort a few miles north called Red River. My Aunt Becky and Uncle Wayne stay there all summer in their motor home. It's a real nice place to visit, and I got to meet lots of folks and their dogs who were there. I always try to give them a big Texas welcome, which is a face/hand lick if they like that sort of thing.

One afternoon, we were sitting by the river that runs through that RV park and got to watching all the ducks swimming along. Now I was on a leash, or might have just given those ducks a good chasing or swimming when we noticed a little bitty dog jump in the river and start swimming toward all those ducks. The current was pretty fast, so he never caught up with any, and then his person noticed where he was and called his name cause he was getting close to a waterfall, and as little as he was, that would have been dangerous if he'd gone over. He turned and swam back to shore and headed off to his campsite. I thought if I'd had a chance I could have caught one of those ducks since I did catch a prairie dog if you remember. We sure enjoyed being in the cool mountain air for a few days. My folks say that playing golf is more fun when the weather is nice, and I agree.

When we got home, three of my girls had had their babies. I was anxious to check on them and make sure all was okay, but of course, they didn't want me to get very close. I speak their language, but that makes no difference when young babes are involved. They know I have to nip at their heels on occasion, so they don't want me around till those young'uns get a little older. It's good that they're protective cause you may remember the coyote incident with Itsy and Bitsy.

Mr. P acted like he was glad to see me. I sure was happy to see him and gave his ears a good washing. I tried to get him to run so I could chase something, but the only thing that entices him to move very fast is food dropping into his bowl. I found LB at the barn, and she acted like I'd never been gone. Course she really doesn't want me to know that she enjoys our chasing sessions. I really think she looks forward to them, so I try to accommodate her as often as I can.

So long,

Kodi

Friend or Foe

Hi Y'all,

Guess what? We finally had, yes, some *rain*. It's been a pretty long while since we've had any more than a shower, so if it hadn't come at night when I was asleep, I might have just stood out in it. I wondered what my girls' babies thought of the wet stuff since some of them are a few months old and have never seen any.

The other night, something happened that made me question my friendship with Mr. P. I guess all good buds have their up and down now and then, but this was the first time that he really ticked me off. It was our night to watch bull riding, so we were all settled in our favorite spots. Daddy was in his recliner, and Mama was on the couch with my head in her lap. I was half dozing, thinking about the popcorn to come later when I noticed Mr. P's tail go by. He jumped up on the other end of the couch and gave me a smirky grin. I wondered what he was up to. Then he made his move, and before I knew it, he was walking on top of me and laid his fat self right on my head so that I had to move or risk being suffocated. It was obvious he intended to have Mama's lap all to hisself. He acted like he was royalty or something. I thought that two could play at this game, so I jumped down and got in Daddy's lap and turned and gave him my smirky grin. He had that "whatever" look on his face and then jumped down and did the same thing to me in Daddy's lap. Then he got down and headed off to his food bowl. I don't think he ever intended to stay either place but let me know that he could shove me out of the way any time he wanted to. I guess all friends have their squabbles, but I want him to know I'm not going to put up with that kind of rude behavior very many times. I know he was here before me, but still I'm head of security around here, and he needs to remember it.

Looks like It'll be a busy fall. We're headed out to Ruidoso for a few days next week for Mama's birthday and then to a cattle sale over in Mississippi after that. "On the Road Again" will be my theme song for a while. I'll let you know how those trips turn out. And since I'll be gone some, maybe Mr. P will miss me, and we'll be back to being friends again.

Kodi

Antlers

Hi Y'all,

Just to let you know so you wouldn't worry—Mr. P and I are best buds again. We were on the outs for a bit, but our friendship survived. Course I've been on the go a lot lately, so that might have something to do with it. They say absence makes the heart grow fonder. When I got back from my most recent trip, he said that he would even play a little with me. I nearly fell over, so I pounced on him, and we had a good tussle. Not for very long, mind you, cause he says a little of me goes a long way. Wonder what he means by that. Anyway it's good to be on his list of friends again. And that thing about putting a restraining order on me was just a joke, and I can get close to him and even clean his ears from time to time.

As I said, I've been on the go, and we just got back from that trip out to Ruidoso. We went there about the same time last year, and we stayed at a place that was right next to a golf course. There was lots of clover in the rough areas, so I got to see lots of deer cause they really like to munch on that stuff. You know those deer were not afraid of me at all. I barked at them from the deck of our condo, and they would just stand there looking at me as if to say, "Bring it on, little dog. We have horns and hooves and know how to use them."

I decided since I didn't know their language like I do my girls, I might better steer clear of them for safety's sake. One group had big horns with stuff called velvet coming off, and it made them look like they had trees on their heads with moss hanging off. It looked kind of funny, but I didn't laugh in front of them since I remembered what they said about those horns and hooves.

We did some hiking up in the mountains while there too. My folks wanted to get out and see the beautiful colors of the aspen trees in their golden glory. I love to go on hikes and get to run and sniff new smells and wade in the cold mountain streams. It's just good to be alive at those times. I know some dogs never get to do the things I get to experience, and I sure am lucky to be one of the ones who do.

After getting back from that trip and getting some chores taken care of, we headed out the other direction to a cattle sale over in Mississippi. That was a new state for me to be in, and it sure was pretty there since they'd had lots of rain this past summer and everything was super green. And it wasn't such a long drive, so I didn't get so road weary.

When we got home, I had the need to do some running and just had to go for it. I ran and ran and ran till my wiggly butt was draggin'. Mr. P has never understood my need for speed. I guess that's one of the differences between him and me, but even though we like different things, we can still be friends.

So long,

Kodi

Limos and Sport Cars

Hi Y'all,

Since my last letter, we've been up to Chimney Rock Cattle Company for their annual cattle sale and gathering. This is my third time to go, and I love getting to see my friends Vegas, Edward, and Zena. In the past, I was kind of leery of Vegas and Edward since my first time there they put me under the truck, but now their huge size and barking's no big deal. Zena is way bigger than me as well, but we have great fun playing. We run and run and run till we're both ready to flop down and chill for a while. Even though she has real long legs, she's no match for my quickness. I have to be quick to avoid the back heels of cows when I'm giving them orders to move. She may be fast on the long stretches, but when it comes to a stop and turn, I can beat her every time. Kind of like I'm a little sports car, and she's a stretch limo.

When we left there, we went to Branson, Missouri, for a short time of R&R, and you know that means some golf for my folks with me riding shotgun protecting the cart from squirrels. We stayed at a condo we'd been at before, but this time, there was this cat that seemed to hang out near one of the other condos. Course me being me, I just had to try to make it run, but it let me know with a growl like I'd never heard before that my face would be rearranged if I didn't leave him alone. I kept my distance after that, but if we were in my home territory, things would have been different, just saying.

I did run across a bunch of new critters one day on the course. At first, I thought they looked like Herkel and Jerkel, but my folks said they were wild turkeys. They loved seeing them and said they sure were big ones. My thought was, *I bet you could get a lot of turkey treats out of just one of those things.* I never know what kind of critter I'll see next on golf courses. I've seen deer, coyotes, prairie dogs, marmots, wild turkeys, and lots of squirrels. Who said golf is for humans? Looks like to me, it's just as much for critters.

And I wonder what the critters think when they're watching humans hitting that little white ball and getting excited when it goes where they want it to. I still think it's a funny game, but I do enjoy riding along in the cart and letting the wind blow my pretty hair.

When we got home, we got back to work separating some pairs from those that won't have their babies till spring. My job was to move that group from point A to point B where the separating would take place, and for once, all was going well except for one baby calf. She's was a real newbie and seemed to have a cold, so I was told to move her and her mom along very slowly. I got behind them and nudged her along at a snail's pace and finally got them to the lot. Daddy grabbed her and gave her some shots to help her feel better. Even though she was little, she still tried to waylay me and Daddy. Those baby calves can be a real handful sometimes.

We're all kind of worried since LB hasn't been around in a while. Now you know she and I are not on the best of terms, but I miss having her around, and I think she really enjoys our chases. I hope she's okay and just off on an adventure cause she's always had kind of a wild streak in her. I kind of miss her trash talking down to me when I put her up a tree too.

So long for now. I'll keep you posted on LB.

Kodi

A New Year

Happy New Year Y'all,

I can't believe another Thanksgiving and Christmas have come and gone, and we're into a new year! I hope all the holidays were special ones for you. I got a big new chewy bone that should keep me busy for a spell. I can go through those things pretty quickly. And I got a new stuffed bear cause mine had sort of lost his stuffin.

I got to visit with some of my doggie cousins too. One is a big yellow Lab named Boo, and we had a grand time running and chasing each other till we were tuckered out. You know I have trouble holding my licker; well, he has trouble not slobbering and got me so wet on my back that I had to have a good towel drying when he was gone.

He has a little sister named Paris who's a real diva. She likes to sit on the couch all covered with a blanket and look down on the rest of us. She's not much into playing, and I guess that's good cause she's kind of old and has the spindliest little legs that definitely couldn't keep up with me and Boo.

I got to wondering the other day if we were going to have any snow this winter. It's the middle of January, and none has fallen yet. I did overhear my folks talking about a possible ski trip later this winter, and that would be a fun time.

It's the time of the year for stock shows, and we just got back from the one at Ft. Worth. My folks love bull riding, but they also love ranch rodeos. I got to thinking that those should have an event for working cowdogs. I mean ranch work would be a lot harder without the help of good dogs like me. Most cowboys don't know the language of *mooooo*, so they have to rely on us to help them talk to the cows. Since us cowdogs provide a valuable service, an event to show off our skills would be a good one to watch.

You know I'm getting concerned about my obsession with chasing things. Now I have other obsessions like my love for popcorn and peanut butter and pouncing on Mr. P when he's napping, but since my old buddy is down in his back and LB's not around, I have to rely on squirrels to take care of my need to chase things, and it may be getting out of hand. And it's really hard for me to stay in the cart when we're on the golf course, and they're running helter-skelter all over the place. They get me so nervous that I get to shaking and whining just at seeing one. And what's really hard is when one comes to the cart and looks at me like "Na na na na, you can't chase me here, can you? He he he."

I mean it's all I can do to keep myself under control, and a few times I haven't been able to. Sometimes I even dream of chasing the furry-tailed varmints and wake up more tired than when I went to sleep. And that's not good cause I need my rest. So if you have any ideas how I might control my squirrely problem, give me a shout. Any help will be appreciated.

Kodi

Barkitis

Hi Y'all,

How's it going? It's definitely winter at this ranch. A few days ago, it was warm enough that Mama opened windows to let in fresh air, and now it's back to bitter cold. Course that means a fire in the den, and that sure makes for good napping. Actually it really doesn't matter to me what the weather is cause I try to enjoy each day as it comes.

My folks have decided that I've developed barkitis. Now that's the opposite of laryngitis, but I guess it could lead to that condition. In my defense, I think my barking is a good way to show the world that I'm head of security around this ranch and not to forget it. Now when I'm indoors, I'm the quiet sort unless the doorbell rings, and then the barkitis comes out. Hey, it's usually only strangers who might ring that bell cause the folks we know come to the back like everybody does out in the country. When I'm outside, I tend to bark at lots of things. Maybe the birds around the bulls' feed trough need talking to, or maybe a truck going down the side road needs to know I'm on duty. When it hits me, I just have to let it out and sometimes my barks bring my folks out to see what I'm upset about. They usually tell me to quiet down since I can be heard in the next county, but they're just joking. Mr. P says he sure could do with less of my barking cause it disturbs his long naps. I don't think it does though; I've seen him stay asleep when I bark right in his ear. I guess you could compare me to a teenage girl who talks a lot on her cell phone and runs up big bills, so it could be worse.

Had a bad cow experience the other day, and my barking nor my understanding of her language didn't help at all. We were out walking in the pasture looking at the newborns when one of my girls got upset with us getting close to her babe and came at us snorting and stomping her feet. I ran and barked at her to get away from my folks, but she didn't and kept coming. My folks threw up their hands and yelled, and she decided to turn and go back to her little one. It was kind of a close call. My girls are good mamas and protective of their young'uns, but she kind of overdid the whole thing. I mean she sees us every day and knows we're the good guys, so why act so mean? And she did the same thing a few days later when it was just me and Mama. This time though Mama had a stick with her, and that changed the cow's mind. Now I can duck and dart fast enough to not be in any danger, but I need to stay close by if my folks are there, so I was glad she thought to bring that stick. That made my protection job a little easier.

Well, so long. I'm sure there's something I need to go bark at—uh, I mean—talk to.

Kodi

Go Away!

Hi Y'all,

Well, looks like it's time to say bye-bye to winter and hello to spring. Everything is gettin' green, and there are flowers all around as well as bees. Since I tend to stick my nose where it doesn't belong sometimes, I'm trying to stay out of the bees' business. This pretty weather sure makes you want to be outside as much as possible before the heat of another Texas summer is upon us.

Been on the go some as if that surprises you. As I've said my name might ought to have been Gypsy. We were at a bull sale recently out at Abilene, and I met the resident sale barn dog. Boy, did he get on my nerves. Every time Mama and I were out walking around, he was right there sniffing me or trying to chew on my ears or just being a nuisance. I played with him some, but he wouldn't let me be when I was ready to stop. The only time I got a break from this pest was when his person needed him to help move bulls up the alleyway, and then Jake would take off. But when he got finished there, here he came again. I guess he meant well and was just being friendly, but a little of him went a long way. I know what Mr. P means now when he says that about me.

A few weeks later, we headed out again down to the Texas hill country. This trip wasn't cattle related but just for fun. Daddy had a birthday, so it was a good time for a short getaway. Besides, my folks wanted to see all the pretty bluebonnets that grow down there. I don't see color as well as humans, so I don't know if they were blue or not, but my folks seemed to enjoy seeing all of them on the roadsides and out in the fields. Course my folks got in some golf and even a little shopping. We went in one store that was devoted to us canines, and I could have stayed in there all day. There were so many different kinds of toys and treats that my mouth drooled just thinking of all the things I could buy. Everyone in the store thought I was a cutie. I still get that a lot even though I'm not a puppy anymore.

It'll be a while before another outing since there's lots of work to do here at home. And the day after getting back, one of my girls had twin baby heifers. She's sure proud of them, and now all the babes are born till those that are due in the fall, so that makes my folks happy.

Well, I'd better go. Remember to take time to stop and smell the flowers that are everywhere this time of the year.

Kodi

Rocks and More Rocks

What's shaking Y'all?

Heard that expression the other day and kind of liked it. Been pretty quiet around here the last few weeks. All the calves are weaned and turned out to grow, and Daddy's been busy with hay season. We've had ample rain this year, so he'll get plenty put up for my girls to eat on this winter. We did take a short trip out to Ruidoso, New Mexico, recently, and that's always a fun time cause it's nice and cool there. One day, we visited a big ranch about an hour from where we were staying. These folks have just gotten into the Brangus business and said if we were ever out their way to drop by for a visit and tour of the ranch. This sure is some rough country, and when we were taking that tour, I thought Mama and I might bounce to death in the back seat of the truck. I think you could walk from rock to rock. I overheard the manager, Tate, say this place used to be a big sheep ranch and that the herders used little dogs like me to help them with their work. Who knows some of my long-lost relatives might have worked here?

It's always good to get away to the mountains even for a short trip. We'll go back later in the summer when it gets real hot here at home. And I needed a break from that crazy mockingbird who's making my life miserable when I'm out back near her nest. You remember I've mentioned her before? Well, she's back. She flies around dive-bombing me with her sharp beak, and I'm getting tired of her rude behavior. I mean I'm not a cat who can climb up the tree where her nest is and bother those babies. Now I'll admit I may have played with one of the babies one time when the little thing fell out of that nest before it learned to fly. But jeez, I didn't hurt it. It just got a little wet from me giving it a good cleaning since you know I can't hold my licker very well. But you would have thought I'd committed murder the way she carried on. And the red birds are back pecking at the windows. I mean the whole bunch has gotten on my nerves. Do they have any sense in those bird brains of theirs? I guess I'll have to put up with all this till their babies fly away, and that'll be none too soon, so a getaway from them was just what I needed for my sanity's sake.

LB is still gone, but I have noticed on occasion recently a big evil-eyed yellow cat lurking around the hay barn. I've ran out there several times barking to let him know he'd better not stray into my yard or he'll suffer the consequences. He's got plenty of places to hide out there, but Daddy saw him too, so now my folks don't think I've lost it when I go out there barking and running in circles. Who knows what he gets away with when I'm gone for several days? I know Mr. P doesn't pay him any mind, so he probably has the run of the place when I'm off duty. But when I'm here, he'd better watch out, just saying.

There's been no alien sighting recently around here, but the other day at our golf course, something spooked me. We were on the ninth fairway when I got out for a run. I just happened to wander into the nearby woods and heard some noises and smelled some things I couldn't quite figure out. It was dark and spooky back in there, and the hairs on my neck started standing up. I looked around but didn't see anything or anyone. I decided I might better mosey back into the sunshine just to be on the safe side. This is not my home territory, so I decided not to tempt fate.

Well, I've been outside lots today in the heat, so I'm ready for some downtime stretched out on the tile floor right under a ceiling fan. Sometimes it's good to be me.

Kodi

OMG! I forgot about the gray hairs I discovered this morning! I was making a patrol around the house and just happened to look in one of the reflective windows, and yikes, I saw some gray hairs mixed in with the shiny black ones. They stood out like a sore thumb too. I couldn't stop looking at them and wondered when more might show up. I'm only three years old, so what will I look like when I'm a senior citizen? I sure don't want to have to start using a hair-coloring product so soon to keep up my youthful appearance. And I know this is not a big deal in the scheme of things, but it sure made me wonder about how I'll handle getting older. I'm used to being super active and everyone saying how cute I am, so I guess I'll just have to roll with the flow and take each day as it comes, gray hairs or not. And I think I'll stop looking in those windows.

Hoppers

Hi Y'all,

Can you believe it's already time to celebrate the USA's birthday again? And I had another one recently too. Seems like yesterday I was saying Happy New Year, and now it's the Fourth of July. I guess when you're a busy little cowdog like me, time has a way of flying by.

Lately I've been enjoying chasing grasshoppers in the yard. They're everywhere, and I love to go after them. I got to wondering what my brainwaves looked like when I'm on the hunt for the hoppers. Now when I'm resting or sleeping, I bet they look kind of like *mmmmmmm* or *zzzzzzzz*, but when grasshoppers are on my radar screen, I bet they go jump, hop, *bzzz*, turn, twist, *bzzzz*, hop, zing, hippity hop. My folks get a kick out of watching me jumping and running after those pesky critters. I got one in my mouth the other day, but I spit it out cause that thing jumped around even in there, and that was kind of weird. I've heard on TV that folks in foreign countries eat those things, and they're quite tasty and crunchy. As for this cowdog, I think I'll stick to my usual diet. Course those foreigners probably don't eat horse hooves that have been buried for a spell, so maybe eating grasshoppers isn't all that bad.

Things are pretty quiet on the cattle front. My girls spend their days grazing, and when it gets hot, they head to shade trees to rest and chew their cuds. Then later in the day, they'll venture back out. Itsy and Bitsy and Stormy are doing fine. Daddy said the other day that Stormy's growing into a fine young bull, and he still likes a head rub when he sees my folks. It'll be a while yet before anything gets weaned, so Mr. P's naps are not being disturbed by any excess noise right now. Course I still like to pounce on him now and then just to have him open one eye and say the usual "Go away, little dog. You're bothering me."

Actually he' s looking out of just one eye right now cause something stung him and his right one is swollen shut. I remember when I got stung, and my face swelled up, so I feel kind of sorry for the ole guy. It hasn't slowed down his eating any, so I know he's all right. He didn't laugh at me when I looked funny, so I'm not going to laugh at his misfortune either. Good friends like each other through good and bad times.

Well, gotta go. It's been kind of hot today, so I feel a nap on the tile floor calling my name.

Kodi

Superpowers

Hi Y'all,

Can you believe that it's already the last of July? Soon we'll be headed back to the mountains for some R&R, and I can hardly wait. Now this summer sure's been better than the last, but a trip to the cool Rockies is always welcomed by yours truly. My girls are sure enjoying this weather, and they're all fat, shiny, and living the good life. Since I speak their language, I often hear them talking about how nice it is to have plenty of grass to graze on and how the pond water is so cool and refreshing. We've had ample supplies of rain lately, so that keeps their water supply just like they like it. And that means there've been lots of puddles to jump and splash in. That's great fun; give it a try some time, and see if you agree.

I got to thinking the other day—I know that won't get me very far ha ha—how nice it would be to have some superpowers. Flying is one that came to my mind first. Since I'm head of security and all, flying would sure come in handy. I could cruise overhead and check on my girls, keep an eye out for invaders like squirrels and armadillos or even aliens. And when we're out in the pasture, I could chase something for a bit and then go airborne and really get it moving. Don't you know those pesky buzzards would take a second look if all of a sudden I took flight just like them? That would be something. I could even have a red cape with a gold *K* on it, and I could have a nickname like the Mighty K. That sounds fitting, don't you think? Well, it was just a thought. What kind of superpower would you choose?

Gotta go cause it's time to move some young bulls away from their feeder. They don't like to leave that free stuff, so it takes some talking to get them to get a move on. If they stay in that trap all the time, they'll just eat and eat and eat, and that's not good for them, so we have to regulate them on their feed intake. They've been pretty easy to train, and they've learned that if they don't move when I say so, some heel nipping is coming next. They try to kick me sometimes, but I'm fast and can duck and dive with the best of them, so I've not been hit yet. Probably will someday though when I get older and slower. Just one of the hazards of my line of work.

Take care and think about that superpower you might want to have.

The Mighty K

Rocky Mountain Paradise

Hi Y'all,

Hope all is well in your neck of the woods. It's hot here because it's August, but that means summer is on its way to being over, and that makes my paws get all tingly just thinking of cool fall days. Course I'm a lucky pup and got to escape to the cool mountains of New Mexico and Colorado on two trips this summer. What a great time we had too! I noticed that other dogs must be lucky like me since there were lots with their people enjoying the mountain air. I did meet two that I didn't care for too much though. They were kind of bullies. We were out hiking, and they came running up at me barking and growling and acting all bad, but retreated when their master called. Now I know how to handle rude cows, but when two of my kind ganged up on me, I wasn't sure if those growls were a joke or not.

And I met a great Dane named Brutus. When he stood up, I got a crick in my neck from looking up at him. I asked how the weather was up there, and he just laughed and said he got that question a lot from little dogs like me. He was a gentle soul though and even lied down so I could talk to him face to face, not face to underbelly. He would have been nice to have around when those two bullies tried to jump me. I bet they would have thought twice before growling at him.

The weather was so nice and cool that being outside was such a pleasure. My folks say that golf or hiking or anything outdoors is so much more fun when you're not trying to keep sweat out of your eyes. Now I don't sweat like humans do, so my panting came from being at high altitudes rather than being hot. That high altitude will tire you out pretty quickly too, and I noticed that falling asleep at night was no problem. Couldn't stay forever though since there's always work to do here at the ranch.

And after being gone a while, it was nice to get back to routines like my morning run, checking on my girls and their young'uns, and pestering—uh, I mean—playing with Mr. P. I think he's even glad to see me after I've been gone for a while, but that wears off pretty quickly. You know how he says a little of me goes a long way.

We were home a while and then went back to Ruidoso for a short spell. We always go out to Westall Brangus Ranch for a visit when we're out that way, and I love to see the manager, Tate. He's a real dog person. He likes to drive us around to see all the bulls and heifers that will be in their fall sale, and it's quite a drive since that place covers 60,000 acres. That's the place where you drive from one rock to another – rough riding.

This time, we had a new adventure. We were about four miles from the headquarters when we heard *kabloom*, and one of the truck tires went flat. Seems as if Tate had run over one of the gazillion rocks out there, and unfortunately, we were out of cell phone service and the tire jack was in the other truck, so our only choice was to start walking. It was rough on my paws and my folks' feet. Mama kept reminding me to stay on the road, too, but that was hard since there were so many smells to investigate. Seems the resident rattlesnakes like to sun themselves on rocks, and she didn't want me sniffing into their business. Luckily two of the ranch hands just happened to come by on their way to fix a water pipe, so we hitched a ride. We were all ready for a cool drink by then, and when we got in the truck and headed back to Ruidoso, I conked out. I guess my adventure finally caught up with me.

The next day, we headed south a way to meet up with Daddy's guide when he goes back out there this fall for an elk hunt. As we were driving along, my folks spotted a herd of wild horses. Mama said that was a new sight as many times as she and Daddy had been down that road they'd never seen any. They were in full run too but finally stopped to graze, and we watched them from the truck. They were smaller than Sug, and I guess that's because they have to fend for themselves in the wild whereas she gets fed daily and of course apple treats. You never know what we're going to see on our trips. It's always an adventure any time we go somewhere.

Guess I'd better sign off for now. I've been out working some today and I'm kind of tired. The cool tile floor seems like the perfect spot for a little nap till dinnertime, and then the couch will be a good spot to spend some time. Mr. P's even welcome to share it with me. Course he hasn't been doing anything that would tire him out, but he's always welcome on my couch.

Kodi

Favorite Things

Hi Y'all,

Hope all is well at your place. No complaints on this end except for it being too hot for my taste. Fall will be here soon though, so I'll need to have just a little more patience. Kind of hard for me.

The other day, I was relaxing. Actually, I was dozing off after my morning run when I got to thinking about all the little things that make me a happy pup. You know I love to run and splash in the edges of the pasture ponds and then run some more. Well, add rolling on my back in the grass to that list. I'll run and run, then plop down, roll over on my back with all four paws in the air, then wiggle and scratch my back. Oh, how good that feels! Here's what you do to get the most out of it: run some figure eights, splash in the edge of a nearby pond, get out and shake, shake, shake, then run some more and fall down and roll on your back, and then wiggle, wiggle, wiggle. Repeat these steps till you're pooped. You don't know what you're missing till you've given this a try.

They say the best things in life are free, and I'll have to agree. Nothing's better than what I just described unless it's coming in from the heat and stretching your belly on the cool tile floor for a nap. Or if it's cold out coming in and getting cozy in your favorite chair with a stuffed toy. Sharing the couch with your best bud is high on my list too. And if Mr. P is in the mood for an ear cleaning, then even better cause you know I have trouble holding my licker. Riding in a golf cart or the mule or the back of the four-wheeler and letting the wind blow my hair is pretty fun too. Chewing on a horse hoof that's been buried for a while or cracking a pecan and getting out that luscious morsel is high on my list. And I sure don't want to forget licking peanut butter out of my Kong or catching popcorn in midair cause I may just be addicted to those two things.

Just thinking about what I've mentioned makes my heart smile. Think about your favorite stuff that takes you to your happy place and tell me about them. I bet you won't have any trouble making that list.

Well, so long for now,

Kodi

PS. I forgot about good friends cause they should always be high on our list of happy things. They sure make life better, don't you think?

Accents

Hi Y'all,

Man, have we ever been busy! For some reason, time seems to speed up this time of the year. I just got back from helping to pen some calves that needed deworming, blackleg shots, and new ear tags to match the brands they'll get pretty soon. Then after they settle down for a week or so, I'll have to help repen them so they can get weaned from my girls. That's always a noisy time around here with lots of bawling and bellowing from them and their mamas. It's kind of sad when you think about it, but it's just part of life. We all go through it, and I survived as did Mr. P. He sure is glad when all the noise dies down some cause I don't think he gets much sleep during that week. His eyes will only half open, and he can be a little grouchy when I pounce on him. But eventually, all will get back to normal, and he'll get back to his twenty-three-hour naps, which he seems to require.

After all the cattle work, we took a long weekend and headed down south to southern Louisiana. Now that's still in the USA, but those folks are called Cajuns instead of Texans like us. And they sound kind of different when they talk too. Now my bark sounds the same no matter where I am, but my folks have been told they have an accent. They sound normal to me though. There are lots of cattle ranches down in that country, and I got to wondering if those cows moo with an accent.

Would I even understand them, and would they know what my Texas bark means like my girls do? Something to think about.

We went down there so my folks could attend a bull riding event. One of their favorite riders was retiring from competition, and this event was held in his honor. As usual, I stayed back in the hotel room while they were out, but I'm used to that, and Mama always leaves my Kong filled with peanut butter for me to enjoy. The downside is that they get to have popcorn while at the event, and I don't get to share in that little pleasure.

Better sign off cause I heard Daddy call my name to head out for our afternoon check of things. Love riding in the mule through the pastures looking at my girls. Sometimes I get out and run a bit and even get in the edge of a pond or two, and as always, Daddy has a treat for me when I get back in to ride. Life is good!

Kodi

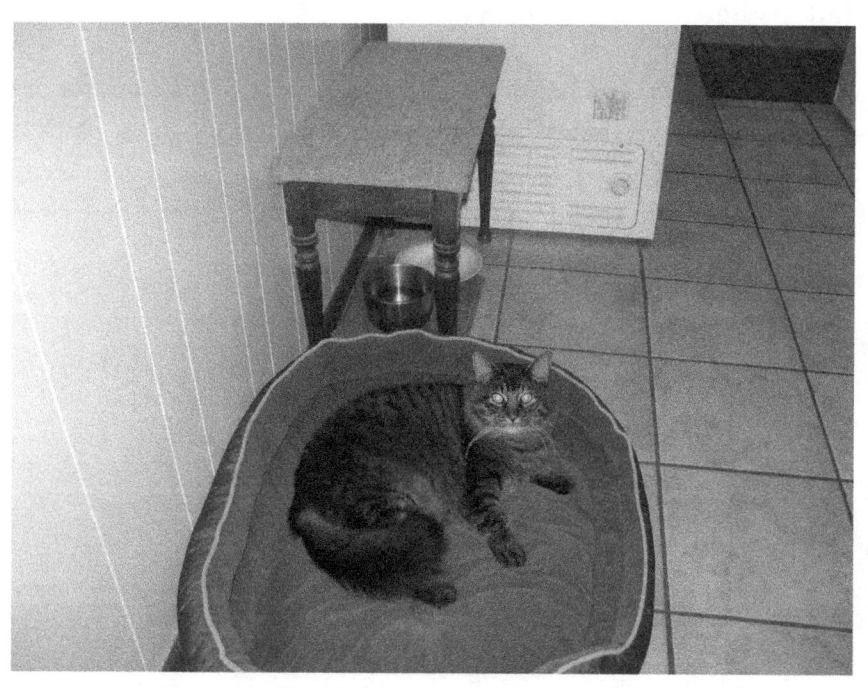

Mean Little Buggers

Hey, hey, hey Y'all,

Fall is finally here! Yeah and double yeah. Now, it hasn't been nearly as hot and miserable a summer as last year's was, but the thought of cool days and chilly evenings make my paws want to do a happy dance. Sometimes on chilly evenings, my daddy will fix a fire in the outside pit, and we'll sit there for a spell. My folks prop their feet up by the fire and enjoy the crackling of the burning logs. I get close by and lie there enjoying it as well. Those sure can be some good times, you know just being with your loved ones not doing a thing but chillin'. Little things like that make the best memories.

Another sign fall is here is the squirrels running here and there gathering stuff to get them through the winter that's ahead. I see lots of them on the golf course but none here at home yet, and that surprises me too since the pecan tree out back is loaded with those luscious nuts. There are so many this year that I guess it would be nice if I shared some of them with the squirrels. I must be getting soft or something cause I usually am not good at sharing food.

You know one reason this past summer wasn't as hot was all the rainfall we've had. But the downside to that is it brings out the fire ants. Have you ever stuck your nose into a fire ant mound? I don't mean on purpose cause that would just be plain stupid but I mean by accident. I've gotten some on my paws before, but the other day, I got stung on my nose and *yeow* isn't a strong enough word to say how that felt! I was following a grasshopper in some deep grass when all of a sudden, he disappeared, so I was nosing around to try to locate him when I managed to stick my nose into a hidden fire ant mound. Those little devils stung me instantly, too, and I drew back my nose in a flash. I rubbed and rubbed it with my paw, trying to get the stinging to stop, but it took a while. I'm sure glad none of those things crawled up into my nostrils and sting me on the inside. I mean a sting on the outside is bad enough, but inside would have been real bad. And what if one crawled all the way to my brain? OMG, I hate to even think about that. I've heard of a "brain freeze" when you drink something real cold too fast, but a "brain sting" would definitely be worse. Fire ants are nothing to be messed with, so avoid them at all costs if you can.

On a more pleasant note, we just got back from a trip out to Ruidoso, New Mexico. We stayed at a house that had stairs, and those things sure are fun to run up and down. Mama says she's glad we don't have them at our house cause I sound like a herd of horses going back and forth. Would be fun though. We got in some golf, hiking, and as always, enjoyed the beauty of the mountains. You know It's good to be me. I get to be a cowdog when needed. I'm head of security. I get to travel and meet now people and their dogs, so as far as I'm concerned, life just doesn't get much better for a little cowdog with a wiggly butt.

Well, so long for now. Be sure and get out and enjoy the beauty that this time of the year brings us.

Kodi

PS. As I finish this letter, my heart is full of tears. My best bud and friend from day one, Mr. P, crossed over the Rainbow Bridge last night. I mentioned a while back that LB had disappeared, and we were worried about her safety. My folks figured something happened to her on one of her adventures as she liked to roam and explore the nearby fence rows and woods. Mr. P acted like he was fine yesterday and ate and slept just like always, but he just didn't wake up this morning. Oh, how I miss him. I know I'll see him again someday when I cross that bridge, but it's hard not having him around right now. RIP, old friend.

The Sleepies

Hi Y'all,

Hope all is well with you and yours. This cooler weather sure is nice, don't you agree? I like being outside more now that the days are not so hot, and I have lots more energy too. You would think that with our morning walk, my daily security activity, and checking on my girls in the afternoon with Daddy that I would be tuckered out by day's end, but with it cooler, I still feel like chasing my Kong toy when it's thrown for me. I will admit though when I come in for the night and get my little belly full of dinner, I do seem to sleep well. I guess exercise and work go hand and hand with a good night's sleep.

You know I mentioned in a recent letter that we had just returned from a trip out to Ruidoso to celebrate Mama's birthday. Well, I forgot to mention we had a collision with a big mule deer on our way home. We were headed out that morning, and all of a sudden out of nowhere, a big buck jumped a guard rail and slammed into the side of our truck. It knocked him down, but he must have been okay cause he got up and ran off into the nearby woods. Our truck was not so good though. There were dents and scratches from front to rear. Now there were deer everywhere in Ruidoso. They were walking down streets like tourists, lying under decks in people's yards, on golf courses, just everywhere. I really would have liked to do a little chasing but my folks said no loud and clear. They reminded me that those bucks have horns and hooves and know how to use them. Now I think I could have avoided getting hurt cause none of my girls have managed to kick me yet since I'm sooooooo fast. But there was no reason to take any chances, and I was on vacation and didn't need to herd them anywhere. I decided that since I didn't speak their language, I best leave well enough alone.

During this time of year, we seem to attend lots of cattle functions, and I wondered if any of you ever get sleepy when the sale is going on. I've noticed that I sure do. When the auctioneer gets to selling, I can't stay awake. First, my ears relax, then my eyelids get heavy, and my head starts to feel like it weighs a ton. I find myself resting it on my paws or Mama's lap. Then I go into la-la land, and I'm out. You would think all that noise from the auctioneer and the ringmen taking bids would keep me wide awake, but it's just the opposite. Now if I were the one bidding, then I imagine I would be on alert cause money would be involved, but that's my folks' job, so out I go. If you see me snoozing—hopefully I'm not snoring—just pass me by. I'll be back to myself as soon as the sale is over.

Thought I would catch you up with what's been happening with Stormy, Itsy, and Bitsy. He's weaned now and hangs out with the other young bulls his age. He's growing and getting ready someday to be a herd sire with his own group of ladies. Itsy and Bitsy are like two peas in a pod. They eat, sleep, and hang out together all the time. You might remember that they were quite small when they were born, but they're growing by leaps and bounds. Their mama's taking good care of them, and they know where the creep feeder is and go in there quite often.

The other day, Daddy called for Mama to look out the kitchen window. Those two were coming up the pasture road side by side, headed to the feeder. When they got their fill, they headed back to the rest of the herd like two little girls holding hands, moseying along. They sure seem to be each other's best friend kind of like me and Mr. P were. But we didn't stay together all the time like they do. I got on his nerves enough as it was; it seemed that a little of me went a long way, or so he said.

By the way, do you have your Halloween costume picked out yet? I really don't understand the whole "try to scare people into giving you candy" thing cause all I have to do is cock my head sideways and look kind of sad eyed, and I get a treat every time. Maybe you should give that a try, and see if you have your folks trained as well as mine are. Anyway, enjoy the holiday and try not to be too scary, and I hope you get lots of loot.

So long,

Kodi

Zzzzzz

Hi Y'all,

Boy, time is sure passing by fast; it's already the end of October. And yes, that means Christmas is lurking on the horizon. Mama says that's evident since one of the stores she shops at already has those decorations out. She thinks that's a little early. How about you?

Went back to my home state recently. We stayed in Branson where we've been several times recently, but I was born just a few hours north of there. I don't remember much about my home area since I was just five pounds of fur when I headed to Texas. I do remember riding in Mama's lap all the way to my new home. And I thought to myself then and there that this new life was going to be a pretty good one, and it sure has been. My folks were pretty easy to train too, since they're suckers for wiggly fur balls with big brown eyes.

While in Branson, I added another thing to my list of "don't like." Gondolas, helicopters, windmills, and roofers banging around on the top of the house are on that list, and now I'm adding ziplines. My folks decided we needed to take a walk down by the river since we had just been at Bass Pro for some shopping, and there was a path that went as far as I could see. As we sauntered along, all was fine till I heard some screaming and yelling and I thought, *There's no cattle around here to get out, and I don't see any wild animals, so what's all the ruckus about?*

Then when we got closer, I looked up and saw people hanging on a cable flying along over the river. Now why would anyone want to do that! And to top it off, Mama said to Daddy that we should do that cause it looked like fun. I thought, *Who is this we you're referring to; don't include me. Never, no way, not me, forget about it.* I mean hanging on to a cable and flying along, does that sound like something a normal person would do willingly? At least when I had to ride on the gondola, I was inside that thing, not hanging on the outside. I thought it might be a good time for me to head back to the truck, but since I was connected to Mama by a leash, I had to keep going. And when we made our return trip, there were still crazies flying by overhead. And music was coming out of the light poles too, and no one was around playing an instrument. I mean what's up with that? I sure was glad to get to the truck and to a safe place.

Not long after that, we headed out to New Mexico to a cattle sale. I've mentioned this ranch before, and I love going out there cause there's lots of room to roam and no ziplines either. We did see signs in town to watch out for bears. We didn't see any, but Tate said that sometimes in the winter, those furry things will come down out of the mountains and play with the floats in the water tanks. Now that would be a sight to see.

Just wondering if you ever fall asleep on the couch and wake up with your folks staring and laughing at you? I did the other night after a long day helping with my girls. I thought, *What's so funny? Haven't you ever seen a dog sleeping before?*

Daddy said I was barking, and my feet were running in place. He said they should have filmed me and put it on YouTube. Hope they don't; that would be embarrassing. Actually that may be the reason I wake up tired sometimes. I mean I'm working during the day and when I'm sleeping. And by the way, I don't make fun of my folks when they fall asleep watching TV. If I could use the phone camera, I'd record them cause sometimes they snore so loudly, they drown out the TV. Just saying.

And another thing, do you know of a good hiding place for half-eaten chewies? Mama doesn't like for me to bury them in the flowerbeds and sure not hide them behind couch/bed pillows. That's definitely a no-no for the neat fairy. I should just finish one off when I start chewing, but sometimes that makes me sleepy, and my eyelids get heavy before I'm through.

All this talk of chewies has me wondering where a half-eaten one might be. I bet one of my horse hoof pieces is just at the right stage for enjoyment. The sun's out, a nice warm breeze is blowing, and I'm in the mood for some chewing. Course that'll probably—*zzzzzzzzzzzzz*.

Thermometers

Hi Y'all,

Well, it looks like it's that time of the year again when we start thinking of all the things we have to be thankful for. My list grows longer day by day, starting with my folks. I'm a lucky pup who's much loved and cared for. Course I kind of figured as much when I first met them and got so many hugs and kisses. I remember my feet weren't on the ground too much at first since one of them kept me in their arms. Now I was leaving a world where my brothers and sisters slept and played with me all day to a place where I would be top dog and have a big furry cat for a best friend. Who would've thought? Sometimes I wonder if my siblings live this good life, travel all over the place, and get to do the work they were destined for. I sure hope so. As always, I'm thankful for PB, popcorn, and chewies, and if a little turkey makes it to my bowl on the special day, well, that'll be just fine with me.

Had to make my annual trip my vet the other day. Do you like going? I'm a healthy sort and only have to go in for my checkup now and then, and I love seeing all the folks at the clinic, but when that exam room door closes, I kind of wish I was somewhere else. That's when I get checked from stem to stern and when I get my temperature taken. Well, that's just wrong on all levels. Now you may get yours checked in a different way, but I get a cold thermometer put in a spot where the sun never shines so to speak. Kind of makes me want to say" hello". Wonder why that thing can't be warmed up some. Then I get my ears, mouth, and teeth checked and of course my weight. That's no biggie since I'm so active that I don't have to worry about the pounds packing on. And that's a good thing or I might have to cut back on my PB consumption. Finally I get my shots, then a treat, and I'm good for another year. If it weren't for that cold thermometer, it would be no big deal.

I've mentioned before that I understand several languages. Of course canine, bovine—had to learn that one in my line of work—feline, that is, if anyone actually understands cats, and equine. But I need to learn some foul because of a nearby rooster. His crowing gets on my nerves when he keeps it up long after the sun is shining in the morning. He lives up the road from our place, but he's a free-ranging fellow and sometimes ranges into our north pasture. He must like to hear himself crow, so I need to be able to tell him to give it a rest since the sun is up and shining.

The other day, my folks had some company, and they were all sitting on the patio when one of them asked what that noise was. I thought, *Hmmmm, you must not have a defective rooster living nearby.*

Well, guess I'd better sign off for now. I just heard my name called, and that means it's time for my afternoon check of my girls. The weather is more to my liking now that it's cooler, so I do more running than riding. Sometimes I've just gotta run.

Kodi

PS. I forgot to mention the UFO I saw out in New Mexico recently. We were at a cattle sale at the big ranch I've mentioned before, and this thing was flying all around. Heard someone call it a drone, but it sure looked like an alien spacecraft to yours truly. They said it was taking pictures of cattle, folks at the sale, and the ranch, but since we were only an hour from Roswell with all those little green men, I'm not so sure.

Mouse Patrol

Merry Christmas Y'all,

Yes, it's that time of the year again. Seems like just yesterday I was thinking of what to put on my wish list, and now Christmas has rolled around again. Course I'm such a lucky pup that I don't really need anything, but if a new chewy finds its way to my toy box, well, let's just say I wouldn't object.

This will be my first Christmas without my BFF Mr. P. I remember the first time when there was a tree all decorated in the den, and he told me to steer clear of it and the presents under it or risk getting sprayed with water. I knew he had been here for a spell, so I did just that. Then one Christmas, he couldn't be found anywhere, but I finally spotted him asleep hidden away among those gifts. When my folks noticed, they got the camera and took his picture. He sure had a grumpy look on his face, too, when the flash woke him up. He looked at me and said, "What? Haven't you ever seen a cat sleeping under a tree before?"

I just snickered and went on my way. Anyway, I hope you get whatever is on your list come Christmas morn.

And before long, I'll be wishing everyone a Happy New Year. I'll be seven years old a few months after that. Before I know it, I'll need help getting in and out of the Ranger. I'll be walking more than running, and my hair will turn gray. Yikes! Guess I'd better enjoy each day as it comes along and not worry about the future.

I'm sure glad there's a group of young bulls in the field behind the house. Why? you might ask. Well, they get fed every morning in two big concrete troughs, and they often leave a few morsels for me to snack on after they mosey off for hay and water. I've developed a real taste for their feed, but I've got to be kind of careful cause that stuff is designed to put on weight, and I sure want to keep my girlish figure. And with me getting older, those extra pounds are a little harder to get off.

Saw a new critter on our morning walk a few days ago. At first, I thought it was just a big ol' bird like Meathead, but this thing flew away as I gave chase and landed in a nearby tree. When my folks caught up, they looked up and said, "Hey, that's an owl. Don't usually see them during the daylight hours as they like to hunt at night."

And from the look on his face, I got the feeling I might be a snack if I stayed around very long, so I indicated we might ought to continue with our walk and leave him be. We were burning daylight, as they say.

And the other afternoon while guarding the pecan tree from squirrel invaders, I spied a little varmint out of the corner of my eye. It was small, gray brown, and very fast. It ran and hid behind the firewood stacked on the patio. I ran over and sniffed and sniffed, trying to get to it, but all I did was upset the stack of wood, and it went rolling everywhere. Mama heard the commotion and came out to see what had happened. The little thing made its escape just then out into the pasture, but she saw it. She said it was only a little mouse and nothing to worry about and that I should try not to scatter the firewood again after she had just stacked it. Now I do remember that mouse patrol was in Little Bit and Mr. P's job description, but now that they're both gone, I guess I'll have to add it to my list. Where's a cat when you need one? I've already got a lot on my plate such as head of security, pecan tree guarder, my girls, bull enforcer, golf cart protector, traveling companion, and now mouse patrol. It's good to be busy, but a pup's got to have some downtime too, so I hope nothing else gets add to my list of duties.

Well, if I don't see you before the new year rolls around, have a happy one.

I know it's a few months down the road yet, but it's never too early to start thinking of a birthday present for yours truly. I don't know if there's a special present for number seven, but you do know how I love popcorn.

Your friend,

Kodi

Mistaken Identity

Hi Y'all,

Can you believe it's already the third month of a new year? And remember this is the month to "beware the ides of March," whatever the heck an *ide* is. And why are we supposed to wear green on St. Patrick's Day or risk getting pinched? Who is that dude anyway and why green? I'd Google those questions if my paws weren't too big for the computer keyboard, and I don't have a cell phone, so if you find out, please send me the info.

Do you ever get mistaken for someone else? Seems like lots of folks think I'm a border collie for some reason. Maybe it's my hair color—I don't know. I'll be out with my folks, and someone will comment on what a pretty border collie I am. I think, *Uh no, I'm a little Aussie. Look, no tail. That's why my kind is referred to as wiggle butts.*

On occasion, some have even rubbed my backside, looking for that tail I don't have. That's when I give them that look that says, "Uh, private area there. OK?" Now BCs are real smart like us Aussies, but I'm not one.

And something else that came to my mind. Do you have a special spot you get in when you're winding down from the day and watching some TV? We sure do in this household. Daddy stretches out in his recliner while Mama gets comfy on the couch with her blankie to help cover her always-cold feet. Now said couch is my chosen spot too, so I try to give her enough room, but sometimes she pushes me with her feet, and I have to move a little. I always look at her with my big brown eyes, and she quits pushing and lets me have all the room I need. And for some reason, about 9:00 p.m., a little bell goes off in my head, and I feel the need to get off the couch and get in Daddy's lap till it's time to go outside for a bit before bedtime. That's our routine. What's yours?

The other night, I got in Daddy's lap at my usual time, and then when it was time to get down, he said to wait a bit as they were still watching a TV show. It was about a band they are fond of, and they wanted to hear the final song. I decided to join in, and Daddy laughed and said I was a bit off key. I thought I sounded okay unlike Mama who can't carry a tune in a bucket as the saying goes. When we're riding along in the truck, she just mouths the words to whatever is on the radio, but when she and I are alone, she sings lout loud, and let me tell you she can't sing, and even my untrained ears can tell that. But that doesn't stop her. I wonder if everyone thinks they sound good according to their own ears. Hmmmm.

I was out back recently watching my girls when I got to missing my old friend, Mr. P. You may remember he crossed over the Rainbow Bridge a while back. Now he was a senior citizen when I came here to live, but he took the time to show me the ropes and would even play some with me even though I was kind of rambunctious. He never even tried to rearrange my face like Little Bit said she would do and thank goodness for that as he was one big feline. I loved to pounce on him when I found him sleeping, which was most of the time. I knew I'd always hear the same thing, "Go away, wiggle butt. You're bothering me."

Once in a while, he would surprise me like the time he came flying around the house and climbed to the top of a tree. I was stunned, but he looked down and said, "What? Haven't you ever seen a cat climb a tree before?"

That kind of activity was rare for him, but if napping had been an Olympic sport, he would have had several gold medals.

So, old friend, if you can hear me, I'll see you someday on the other side of that bridge, and I'll expect you to be waiting for me. Course I'll have to pounce on you just to hear those familiar words one more time.

All this sleeping talk has me thinking a nap might just be the thing to do right now. The sun's out, and a soft breeze is blowing, and nothing needs my attention at the moment. Who knows? Maybe I'll dream of that big old cat and all the fun we had during our time together.

Kodi

Kerflop

Hi Y'all,

Spring's here, and the flowers are in bloom. My daddy's had his birthday, and I'll be having one soon. May 20 just in case you forgot.

Spring's sheddin' time, too. Now I get a good brushing pretty often cause I have lots of hair, but during sheddin' season, that doesn't help too much. When Mama runs the vacuum cleaner, the holder fills up pretty quickly, and it seems to have lots of my hair in it. And it's not only me doing the sheddin'; when Sug trots by, you can see the hair falling off her. Then before long, her pretty dark red coat will be super shiny again. And my girls are getting their shine on again too after the winter.

I wonder if all pups are on the go as much I seem to be this time of the year. Now I love to travel, and that's good as spring is a busy time with cattle events to attend as well as other things. My folks like to go to music concerts, and we've attended several already this year. And this is kind of embarrassing, but if you can't laugh at yourself, then who can you? On a recent hotel stay, I actually fell off the bed in the middle of the night, and I didn't land on my feet either. Thankfully, that bed wasn't as high as the one here at home. I was sound asleep, and I guess I rolled over and was too close to the edge, and the next thing I knew, I went kerflop right on the floor. Woke my folks up too as well as yours truly. They checked to see if I was okay, but the only thing I hurt was my pride. I mean who falls off a bed? I bet the folks in the room below us wondered if the sky was falling.

Wonder why there's one in every crowd determined to be different. I've only been in this cattle business for a few years, but I've seen it happen again and again. One of my girls had twin bull calves recently, and every day when I'm riding with Daddy in the Ranger, making a check of things, one of those little toots is always off by hisself. Then we have to drive and drive and drive till we find him. When he's located, we get out and try to head him in the direction of his mother and brother. That's all well and good till he starts bawling like we're trying to hurt him, and here comes his mama, and she's never in a good mood. And of course I get lots of *moooooo* abuse just for trying to be helpful. I head for the safety of the Ranger, and she rounds up her little delinquent, and off they go.

Sure would be easier if those two would stay together like Itsy and Bitsy always did. Those two were never apart. They nursed together, ate creep feed together, and even napped together. When I spotted one, I knew they would both be there, but these two little guys are different. Daddy named them Pete and Repete, and I bet you know which one is the problem child. Hopefully when he gets older, he'll realize he supposed to be a herd animal, not a loner, and will stay with the others. Sure will make my job easier.

Guess I'll say adios for now. It's a beautiful day, and if I knew how to fish, I might just wet a hook. But toy chasing would be just as good. I think I'll go find Mama since she's outside doing some yard work. If I cock my head just so and look at her with my big brown eyes, she'll know I want to chase my toy for a spell. She'd drop what she's doing and go get it and give it a few throws. I wonder if other humans are as easy to train as mine have been.

Kodi

Ears

Hi Y'all,

Whew, but it's been hot lately! Now I know that's the way Texas summers are, but I'm sure glad that fall is on the horizon. Thankfully, this time of the year, there's not much cattle work to do, so I get to spend lots of my time indoors with my little belly stretched out on the cool tile floor. And my girls are smart enough to stay in shady areas during the heat of the day, so we do our checks early or late. It won't be long though before the fall calvers will start having babies, and I sure hope it will cool some by then.

I got to noticing something the other day and wondered if you had. There sure are lots of different kinds of ears. When I was a pup, one of mine would pop up when I got excited, and my folks jokingly called me Radar. Mr. P's ears seemed to stay up all the time even when he was sleeping, which was most of the time. He said that was so he'd know when I was going to pounce on him. Sug's ears are always upright, but that may be cause horses are flight animals and always have to be aware of danger so they can run if necessary. I have notice hers do seem to stand up straighter though when Mama whistles, and she knows it's time for her apple treat. Now my girls ears are big and floppy, but that's partly because of the kind of cattle they are, Brangus.

You may remember a while back I mentioned a twin calf named Itsy whose ears were so big compared to the rest of her body that I thought she could fly if she could flap those things fast enough. Mr. Donkey-in-the-Next-Field has huge ears, and I thought he might be useful in early alien detection, but so far, that hasn't been the case. Now human ears look pretty much the same to me except some have stuff dangling from them called jewelry, but not all. And some even have phones attached to them, and that looks just plum goofy to me. Surely they take those things off now and then. Anyway I wondered if you had taken notice of ears lately.

Ever had one of those mornings when you just didn't want to put one paw in front of the other? That's how I felt a few days ago and don't know why. I didn't want to do any running on our morning outing, and I wasn't hungry either. When I left my breakfast in my dish, my folks knew I didn't feel good. And my nose was warm when it's supposed to be cool and moist. They decided I better make a vet visit and get a checkup. Since I'm usually pretty healthy, I only have to go once a year and truthfully by the time we got there, I was perking up. My doctor gave me the onceover though, and everything checked out. I even got that cold thermometer used on me, which is not my favorite thing. Since then, I've been my usual frisky self, so who knows what was wrong that day?

We've been on some outing lately. One trip was to Alabama to a cattle event. The man who bought possession of our bull Texas Star had a gathering at his ranch, and it was good to see Tex again, and he sure looked like he was living the good life. Later, we headed out to Ruidoso for some R&R and a visit to our friend Tate's place. I love those mountain trips, especially since it's way too warm for my taste here at home. When we do some hiking and I get to wade in the cold mountain streams, well, it just doesn't get any better than that.

I just heard my name called, so it's time for our afternoon check of things. I saw Daddy get a treat out of the jar and put it in his pocket, so I'll get that later. Now riding along with the wind blowing my fur is special enough, but if it makes him happy to give me a treat, then who am I to deny him that happiness?

So long and happy trails to ya. Stay cool and think fall.

Kodi

What a Day!

Hi Y'all,

September has finally arrived, and none too soon for yours truly. It hasn't been as hot a summer as the bad one a few years back, but the thought of the cool days of fall make me want to do a happy dance. And since this is Mama's birthday month, I'm sure we'll take a trip somewhere about that time. I overheard my folks mention Branson, so I'll let you know.

The other day when Mama was out with Sug, I noticed that something was different, and then I realized her pretty tail was lots shorter than it was the day before. Mama used to show horses in competition, so she likes to keep Sug all groomed and pretty just like she was headed into a show ring. Anyway, Mama noticed the short tail and said she bet those rascally calves had gotten it in their mouths kind of like a pacifier and chewed it off. Sug is such a gentle soul that she just stands there when resting and lets those calves lick and rub all over her. Now there's still enough to swat at flies, but it looks kind of funny. That would never happen to me since I don't have one of those things hence the nickname Wiggle Butt, but I can see where tails can be useful. Fly control or helping with balance comes to mind, and Mr. P would use his to curl around his face when it was cold, but I manage just fine without one. My cousin Boo has a big one that can clear off the coffee table when he gets excited, and he's so big and clumsy, it may help him to go straight

159

when we're running. Even without one, I can still run circles around him though.

Well, it finally happened. Yes, I hate to admit it, but I got kicked by one of my girls, and I do mean *kicked*. Now it may have been a little bit my fault, but she didn't have to lambast me so hard. Mama has said for years that it was going to happen if I didn't quit getting so close to their back heels, but in my line of work, that's just part of the job description. On that particular afternoon, Mama and I were out walking in the pasture near a pond. I went in for a drink and a cooldown, and my girl was getting a drink a way down from me. I got out and, as usual, felt the need to run, and that I did. As I went behind her, I guess I startled her, and she kicked out and caught me off guard. I tumbled over and over down the pond embankment. And as I was trying to get up, she ran over me on her way to join the rest of the herd. I thought, *Jeez, couldn't you have gone another way?*

Mama saw all this from a distance and came running. I wasn't hurt much except for my right front paw that she stepped on, and I was sore for a few days but nothing major. I learned a lesson though: don't startle a drinking cow if you're behind her.

And to top the day off, a red wasp stung me on the tip of my nose while I was resting after the kicking ordeal. I mean I was just lying there, and it landed right on my nose and gave me a good sting. Some days it doesn't pay to leave the house.

Guess I'd better go. I see some of the newbies out running around in the field behind the house, and they might want to play some. I think I'll mosey over there, and see if they'll let me join in. Hopefully their mamas won't object and come after me cause with the luck I've had lately, I might just end up in a cast. Take care, and let's hope fall weather stays around for a while.

Kodi

Trapped

Hi, y'all,

Fall is here and the word *yeah* comes to my mind. I always like seeing summer temperatures in my rearview mirror as the saying goes. This past one wasn't as bad as some, but any hot weather is too much for yours truly. Mama said she's glad she can open the windows and let in the fresh air, and Daddy loves to build a fire in the outside pit in the cool evenings. I kind of like that myself. Oh, we didn't get up to Branson, but did go out to Ruidoso for a spell, and I was wondering if you had ever seen a sled dog team made up of Chihuahuas? One morning while on a walk, this man had six of the little tykes, and they were pulling him along at a pretty rapid pace for such little dogs. As they trotted by, he laughed and said they were his sled dog team in training. My folks got a chuckle out of that, and Mama said she could just see the six of them pulling a tiny sled through the snow with an elf shouting, "Mush, you little terrors! Mush!"

All I could think of was them trying to work cattle, and that image was pretty funny to me. Course they would have to learn the language of *mooooo*, but I bet my girls wouldn't pay much attention to such tiny critters.

I've decided that there must be an unwritten law somewhere that something is bound to go wrong when moving cows from point A to point B. Does it seem that way to you, or is it just at our ranch? Daddy said the other morning that we needed to move the west-pasture bunch to another field for some fresh grazing. We got them started off down the pasture road, and Daddy went ahead to open the gate while Mama and I stayed behind to keep them moving. I was going back and forth just like always when I noticed three cows veering off to the left, and before Mama and I could stop them, they crossed a creek and headed back to where they had just been. She and I took off running as fast as we could, and that was not easy in deep wet grass, but we finally got to them and got them started back toward the rest of the herd. We were pooped by then, and I thought, *Why is there always one cow determined to do just the opposite of what she's supposed to, and she always manages to take a few other cows with her?*

I speak their language but have never gotten an answer to that. I guess that's a secret in the cow manual that they don't want to share with this wiggle butt. When we finally got them where they were supposed to be and counted, we headed to the house, but that was a pretty long walk, so you can believe I was ready for a nap after getting cleaned up.

Oh, I got to wondering if you ever watch reality shows on TV. My folks watch several like *American Pickers* and *Mountain Men*, and I got to thinking that my life might just make for good reality TV. A crew could follow me around and record what happened here at the ranch or on our travels. I bet lots of other canines and maybe even felines would tune in each week just to see what was happening. If I could use the computer, I would pitch that idea to the executives at Animal Planet or those guys on *Shark Tank*. Sometimes my ideas just amaze me. I've even got a title, *The Adventures of Kodi the Little Texas Cowdog*. How does that sound?

Well, so long for now. Think about my TV show idea and let me know what you think.

Kodi

PS. I forgot to mention something that happened the other day, and I hope you'll keep this to yourself e I'm pretty embarrassed to admit that I got trapped in the barn by that evil yellow cat I mentioned earlier. Mama and I were outside, and as usual, I made a run to the hay barn to let any intruders know I was still in charge around here. I went in a tunnel between some hay and the side of the barn wall, and when I turned to come back out, guess who was blocking my path? Yes, that evil, hissing, mean-looking yellow cat. I stopped in my tracks immediately. Mama was calling my name, but I didn't even want to bark to let her know where I was. Finally, Daddy came out, and she told him I was somewhere in the barn, but she couldn't understand why I wouldn't come out. Daddy went to the back and noticed that I had been trying to dig my way out there, so he got something and pried a panel loose so I could escape. Whew! Mama said she saw that evil cat and agreed he was nothing to be messed with. Boy, was I glad to see the light of day again and was lucky not to have had my pretty face rearranged by that hissing thing. Now don't think I was scared, but I decided to err on the side of caution and leave that evil thing alone.

Happy Trails

Hi Y'all,

Hope all is well in your neck of the woods. Things couldn't be better around this ranch. Plenty of grass for my girls, and cooler temps sure make this little cowdog one happy camper. Speaking of camping, you know I'm on the go a lot, and I love all the traveling, but lately, some of our trips have taken on a new twist since my folks got an RV. It's like we're taking our house with us where ever we go. At first, I wasn't too sure I was on board with this thing since I didn't like the steps to get in and out, but now I'm getting used to it. And I like the places we park it cause there's lots of room to get out and roam. Also there's always plenty of people to meet and greet, and most of them have their fur babies with them as well. So don't be surprised if I see you at some campground, and if I do, I'll be sure to give you my big Texas howdy, which, as you know, is a good hand or face licking.

Just wondering if you have a routine that you don't like changed. Well, I sure do. Every evening for a kind of dessert, I get a special chewy made from peanut butter that just melts in my mouth—sooooo gooood. And in the mornings when we get back from our walk and if I don't have some work to do, I head to my folks' bedroom and take a little nap in my favorite chair. Well, the other morning, not paying much attention to things, I jumped in said chair, and it started rocking! I got out in a flash and looked back and realized Mama had put a new one in its place. She was standing close by and thought the switcheroo was kind of funny. Not me. I looked at the new chair and then at her and thought, *What the heck! It was here yesterday, so where did my chair go?*

Mama said, "Kodi, I moved your chair to that other corner, so just go nap over there." Well, I saw my old friend, but it's just not the same. I mean the light's different in that corner, and my view of the TV is not how I like it. Routines—if it ain't broke, don't fix it!

Sug got her hooves trimmed the other day, and that meant four little treasures for yours truly. I got each one as the farrier cut them off and headed off to find a good hiding spot. I like to save at least three for later chewing. Just as I got the third one buried, I got the feeling that I was not alone in the shrubbery. And then something with real long ears and a cottony tail jumped out and took off. I was kind of startled, so I just stood there for a bit, but then I took off in hot pursuit. Man, that thing could run, and you know I can too, but he was long gone into the big hay barn before I caught up with him. I guess as long as he leaves my treasures alone, he can stay around, but if he starts chewing on them, then we'll have to have a serious discussion. Seems as I get older I'm getting more tolerant of critters invading my territory, but my patience only goes so far.

Guess I'd better sign off. Always something that needs my attention. Sug might want to visit, or there might be some leftover feed in the bull troughs. Oh, I just heard my named called, so it's time to go for our afternoon check of my girls, and that means a treat. Life is good.

Happy trails to ya,

Kodi

PS. I forgot to mention my new feline friend. The other afternoon, we were by the fire pit winding down the day when all of a sudden, a long black kitty wandered up. He acted like he was home, so my folks said,

"Looks like we've been adopted." Mama went and got him some food, and he's been here ever since. He seems real familiar too and is very friendly. I asked him where he came from and why he came here. He said he was kind of homeless and had this dream one night that if he came to our ranch, it'd be a good place to live. In this dream, a big fat—uh—fluffy cat said he'd have plenty to eat and always be safe and taken care of. I got to thinking, *A big furry cat told him all this? Hmmmmmm.*

And to top it off, he even knew to call me Wiggle Butt and tell me to quit bothering him as he was trying to nap. Kind of strange, don't you think?